<u>BESIEGED</u>

By Jason Winstanley

For Alli and Dan, and my Mum

And for my Grandma, Sheila Corfield, who always thought that I would one day write a book

Besieged

Hannigan

Dusk was falling across the enormous park. Steve Hannigan always felt that it crept up quickly in this part of the world, the high heat of the late afternoon morphing seamlessly into early evening. Cocktail time. Beer o'clock. Not right now, though. Geddes gave him the countdown signal and he prepared to begin his piece to camera.

He'd positioned himself so that the bulk of the crowd was behind him; it seemed restless tonight, but so far peaceful. After almost a week of covering these protests, he was beginning to be able to sense the crowd's mood, as though it were a living, breathing entity with its own emotions, rather than a loose assembly of thousands of disaffected citizens. On previous nights, he'd felt that the mood had been uglier, more provocative and, sure enough, on those evenings, there had been some scuffles and some arrests. The atmosphere tonight was strange - tense and expectant. He wondered if Geddes felt it too. He'd have to ask him later. He imagined them swapping war stories over beers in the hotel bar; it was good to see him again.

Geddes gave the thumbs up from behind his camera and Hannigan launched into his report, explaining the background to the crisis yet again to the viewers of Planet News Network. He was on familiar ground here, but the stalemate was beginning to present him with a challenge – how to be able to find new angles to the story whilst still presenting his viewers with the basic facts they'd need to understand the situation. So he went through his rote once more, explaining in less than a minute how the protests had started up just over a month ago, initially in the universities, and then spreading to the general populace. He quickly described how the initial disgruntled opposition to the government's curbs on free speech had developed into organised mass protest, paralysing whole sections of the city for hours at a time. He finished his background piece by pointing out, as he always did, the fundamental contradiction between the authoritarian approach adopted by the country's government and the frenzied orgy of commerce which was the city's lifeblood.

And then he was onto new material, explaining how the government had responded to the unrest by earlier today enacting even more draconian powers. It had been a show of strength but Hannigan knew it was likely to only inflame the situation, and he gave his viewers the benefit of his opinion. Behind him, the crowd pulsed and there was sporadic chanting. A thin line of blue-uniformed police officers stood impassively in front of the protesters. Hannigan knew this would make for good TV, that the rancour of the crowd would be manifest against the dramatic background of the setting sun. But he also knew that, unless something exciting happened, his reports would start to slip down the schedules at PNN. As Dave Geddes gave the signal to cut, Hannigan found himself wishing that something, anything, would give. It just needed that little spark, a catalyst, to ignite the smouldering resentment into something bigger, much bigger, and when that happened, he would be there to report it.

They started to pack up their gear. The light was fading quickly now and the crowd was starting to disperse, the tension which had previously filled the air starting to evaporate. As the two men walked out of the park, Hannigan looked over his shoulder to where a handful of hardcore protesters were still lingering. This is a city on the edge, he thought.

The Hotel

The hotel was situated at one end of the island that the city sprawled across, close enough to downtown and the harbour to be convenient to its affluent clientele, but far enough away to offer a small oasis of relative calm amidst the hurried business being conducted across the great metropolis. Like any building worthy of note in this city, the hotel had its own tower, but unlike most of the others, this one was shrouded in temporary cladding and an intricate network of scaffolding. An enormous banner stretched across a portion of the scaffolding informed passers-by that the hotel was re-inventing 5-star luxury but that, in the meantime, it was still open for guests. Alongside the tower and adjoining it, although squat by comparison, sat the hotel's original building, a handsome three-storey brick edifice, dating back to colonial days.

A liveried concierge opened one of the large smoked glass doors. Hannigan nodded to him as he and Geddes stepped inside, instantly feeling the welcome cool wash of the air conditioning as they entered the plush lobby. To their right, an open doorway gave to a casual bar and lounge area. The two men exchanged a quick, knowing, glance and then, without a word between them, turned towards it.

*

Hannigan took a swig from the foamy beer and then turned to his colleague, raising his glass.

"Cheers, good to see you, buddy."

Geddes clinked his own glass against Hannigan's.

"Still the same thirsty old Steve then?"

"No change there, my friend." Hannigan patted his considerable paunch. "All bought and paid for."

Geddes grinned, "Yeah, mainly on expenses."

Hannigan grinned back. "Screw you, asshole."

They wandered away from the counter and found a couple of easy chairs within the hotel bar.

Hannigan took another sip of his drink. "Seriously, though, Dave, it really is great to see you. Great to be working with you again."

"Likewise, Steve."

The two Americans were comfortable in each other's presence, as though the two years since they had last seen each other were more like two days.

As they sat down, Geddes asked, "So what happened to the other guy?"

"What other guy?"

"The other cameraman. How come they asked me to get my ass out here, pronto?"

"Oh, Mike. Yeah, good guy," Hannigan took another swig of beer and wiped his mouth with the back of his hand. "Got called back Stateside. Family emergency, apparently."

Geddes shrugged. "Shit happens, huh? Still, it's an ill wind and all that. At least it's brought us back together again."

Hannigan gestured around the bar, "Yep. A little bit more luxurious than Somalia, though, huh?"

Geddes chuckled. "And then some."

He looked around approvingly. "Yeah, seems like a nice place."

"Oh yeah," Hannigan settled back into his easy chair, cupping his beer glass comfortably inside his large palm. "It's been good stayin' here this past week. They got building work going on, but you wouldn't really know it – they only work during the day, keep reasonable hours. They're givin' that big tower a complete overhaul."

Geddes nodded. "I saw that from the street."

"It's gonna be amazing when it's finished – apparently, they're building all sorts into it; restaurants, running tracks, rooftop pool. The works."

Geddes smiled. "Shame this didn't all kick off in six months, then. Place sounds like it's gonna be kinda cool."

Hannigan shrugged his broad shoulders. "I guess, but this is plenty good enough for me. They got this bar area open, the ground floor pool and the best bit... not many guests. They got three floors open, that's all. Maybe fifty rooms - that's only a hundred or so guests. You come back in six months, buddy, place is gonna be crawling with people."

"Maybe." Geddes took a swig of his beer. "But, like you say, helluva lot better than Somalia."

"I heard you've been in a few hotspots since," said Hannigan, a trace of envy in his voice.

"Can't stay away, Steve. Syria, Iran, Venezuela. You know how it is."

"Yeah, I've missed all this, these past couple years."

"Washington?" asked Geddes.

"Yeah. White House correspondent. OK, so it's a promotion, looks good on the resumé but Christ, it's dull. Biggest danger's fallin' asleep in one of the press conferences. It's this stuff that I live for. I missed the action."

"I can understand that," said Geddes, taking a sip of his beer. Behind him, a large and ornate standard lamp cast a muted glow, illuminating his silvery hair. "So how did you get away? Get away from DC and the suits and back to this?"

"Gave 'em an ultimatum they couldn't refuse."

"Which was?"

"Put me back into foreign affairs and I'll take a pay cut."

"Jeez, great negotiation skills, Steve! How'd Mary take that?"

Hannigan looked sheepish for a moment. "Badly."

A silence hung heavy between the two men for a few seconds. Then Geddes said, "That's why the freelance single life suits me. Nobody to answer to but yours truly."

Hannigan took another gulp of his beer, feeling guilty as he realised that he envied the cameraman and his uncomplicated lifestyle.

Geddes checked his watch. "Well, Stevie..." he downed the rest of his beer, "been a long day. Gonna check in and hit the sack."

"No problem, my man."

Hannigan stretched out his big, black paw of a hand and gripped Geddes' smaller, white, palm.

"See you tomorrow, Dave."

"No problem."

As Geddes left, Hannigan signalled to the lanky barman for another beer.

<u>Happy Families</u>

Graham Brazier's feet were aching. He was also sweating profusely, and in need of a drink. The heavy plastic bags of shopping that he was carrying were beginning to cut into his hands. For a moment, he shifted all of the bags to his left hand and examined his right palm. An ugly white line cut diagonally across it, seemingly seared in. Redistributing the weight of the bags yet again, he paused as they reached a road. An apparently endless stream of traffic poured past, yellow taxis mingled generously with the cars and vans. Overhead, a huge plane lumbered its way in towards the airport.

"It's just down there on the left," said Tricia, pointing in the vague direction of their hotel.

"Thank god for that," said Gaby sullenly, brushing a strand of her fine, brown hair from her eyes. "This is total shit."

Tricia rolled her own eyes, and almost literally bit her tongue. Bitter experience had taught her that responding to her fourteen-year-old daughter would almost certainly result in an argument. Graham, though, wasn't so circumspect.

"Hey, watch your language," he snapped.

Gaby let out a sigh and folded her arms across her chest. "I'm really hot and I need to sit down. OK?"

Graham shook his head. "Don't you think we're all hot and bothered? It's not all about you, you know."

Gaby shot him a spiky glance.

"Don't take that tone with me," snapped Graham.

"What tone? All I did was look at you."

"Come off it, Gaby, you know what I mean."

"This day has been sooooo long."

"Don't be so ungrateful, you..." Graham caught himself, just in time. He'd been about to use a descriptor for his stepdaughter which would have seen this argument descend to whole new, and unnecessary, levels.

"Please – can we not do this?" implored Tricia.

"I'm just saying that Gaby should be grateful that we are here, in a place where most of her friends would give their eye teeth to go to, we've spent the whole day shopping, and a little sight-seeing, and she just needs to appreciate what she's being given."

"That's right, talk about me like I'm not here," said Gaby pointedly.

"I just meant…"

"Oh, please!" cried Tricia.

An uncomfortable silence settled as the three of them waited for the pedestrian crossing to turn green; it did, and they crossed the road wordlessly, and continued that way till they reached the hotel. Graham fumed silently. What should have been a great first day of their trip had turned into one of testy, spiteful exchanges between him and his stepdaughter, with sporadic tearful interjections from his wife. He glanced across at Tricia and Gaby; both were steadfastly marching towards the hotel, heads defiantly facing forwards, conversation unsought and unwanted. Wrapped up in their morose thoughts, none of them registered the distant chanting coming from the other side of the city.

*

The Braziers' collective mood had not improved by the time that they returned to their small suite of rooms. Shopping bags were dumped melodramatically, Gaby flounced into the bathroom and slammed the door shut, and Tricia collapsed onto her bed, let out a huge sigh and started to massage her eyes. Graham Brazier shook his head, opened the doors to the balcony and headed outside. After an agitated few seconds, he came back inside, went to his suitcase and rooted through the contents until he found what he was looking for. Then he went back out onto the balcony.

Several seconds later, Tricia, still prone on the bed, felt her nostrils twitch. "Graham," she called, "Are you smoking?"

There was no answer.

"Graham?"

"OK, yes, I am," came the reply from the balcony, "I just really needed one."

"But you're supposed to be giving up."

Out on the balcony, Graham took a final drag of his cigarette, and exhaled. The city spread out before and beyond him. From this vantage point on the third floor of the old building, he had a pretty good view – of skyscrapers all around, of a hazy late afternoon sky, and the harbour, efficiently busy and iconic in equal measure. Far beyond the harbour, he could glimpse the ocean proper, twinkling under the soporific sun. Cruise liners and cargo ships were out that way.

Reluctantly, he stubbed out the smoke and called through to Tricia, "OK, I've stopped then."

Disregarding the ashtray which had been thoughtfully provided on the balcony's table, he instead flicked the remains of the cigarette off the balcony. He watched as it tumbled down until he lost sight of it as it dropped towards the street.

He thought about being back home, catching the train and doing his hour-and-a-half commute to London through the East Midlands countryside on his screamingly expensive rail season ticket. He imagined getting off at Kings Cross and then getting the Northern Line to Old Street, the five minutes it then took him to walk to the office right in the middle of cool-as-fuc

Shoreditch. The young guys who worked there, with their bushy beards, zippy scooters and almond milk. And then there he was, a portly, balding fish out of water, years past his prime – if he'd ever had one - and looking forward to… what, retirement? If he clung on that long. His face didn't fit any more, he knew. At least his knowledge and experience still counted for something, but he was clinging on by his fingernails, and he knew it. And, if they "let him go early" – then what? The fat monthly pay-check, the welcome annual bonus… where would someone at his time of life be able to replace those? He shivered a little despite the humidity. There was always agency or interim work, he supposed. But in his mid-fifties? He thought about the disruption to his life that that kind of peripatetic existence would bring. He could cope with his long London commute, and he had no problem staying a couple of times a month in the mid to upper range hotels, as required by his current role. But doing so on a semi-permanent basis? He imagined being in a budget hotel on the outskirts of some godforsaken city in the middle of nowhere, living out of a suitcase all week before heading home on a Friday afternoon to Tricia and a dog's load of abuse from Gaby. He tried to imagine the journey home, on either a packed motorway or a packed train, grey skies and rain lashing the windows. God, was that what he had to look forward to? He closed his eyes, and vaguely registered some noise coming from across the city.

As head-clearing sessions go, this one hadn't been a success. He had come out here feeling angry and frustrated; now he was just feeling morose. He gripped the rail of the balcony with both hands and stood for a moment, with his head bowed. Jesus, he thought, what a great start to the holiday. And we haven't even met up with Colin yet.

Relaxing his grip on the rail, he straightened up and moved back into the room; Tricia was still lying on the bed and the bathroom door was still well and truly closed. The closed door suddenly made him aware of just how full his bladder was getting. Ignoring the feeling, he collapsed onto his own half of the bed and stared at the ceiling. A small crack ran from the join with the wall to where the main light fitting was situated. For a moment, he lay there, and felt the gentle, cool pressure of the air conditioning on his skin. He imagined the humidity of the city being wafted away from him, of his stresses and pressures going the same way. He lay very still and could feel the pulsing of his own blood in his ears and temples; but the pressure on his bladder was growing more intense. Reluctantly, he hauled himself off the bed. He glanced down at Tricia; her deep breathing told him that she had fallen asleep.

Softly, he knocked on the door of the bathroom, "Gaby," he whispered urgently, "sorry, but are you going to be long? I need the bathroom."

There was no answer, so he knocked again, a little more insistently.

"Gaby? Sorry, I need…"

"What Graham? I'm busy in here, for God's sake!"

"I just need to know if you're going to…"

"I said I'm busy!"

Inside the bathroom, Gaby was sitting on the floor. She drew her knees up to her chest and wrapped her arms around them. Mindlessly, she blew out a bubble of saliva as she stared at the bath. The bubble burst with a little pop but she didn't notice.

Gaby had no clue what her mother saw in Graham. Like, literally, no fucking clue.

God, but he was such a jerk. A fat, bald jerk too. Pretty rich, though. That must be what her mother saw in him, and she felt herself starting to hate her a little bit for it. Which made her hate herself a little too. She did love her mum; if only she hadn't gone and made such a stupid choice three years ago.

Three long years ago.

And now here she was, on the other side of the world, for three freaking weeks. Her friends back home would be going on days out – theme parks, cinema, shopping, coffee shops, messaging each other and watching YouTube – all without her. She wished she hadn't left her phone in the suite; she really needed to WhatsApp Olivia or Hannah or Daisy, but that would mean giving up this little sanctuary. And she couldn't face seeing Graham again. Or she could message her dad. She wondered what he was doing right now, and where in the world his ship was. She didn't even know what time it was in his part of the world. He might be fast asleep for all she knew, or in a really cool city. He might even be coming into the harbour on the other side of the road from the hotel. As she thought about that unlikely prospect, she felt tears welling up in her eyes, and a plump wetness trickled down her cheeks.

On the other side of the door, Graham Brazier shrugged his shoulders, took a quick look at his sleeping wife, and then picked up his room key and wallet, quietly opened the door, and headed for the hotel bar.

Oleksanders

The lift reached the ground floor, and Graham Brazier emerged, along with a portly American woman, whose pungent perfume would no doubt linger in the lift for hours. Stepping out into the lobby, he was once again taken, as he had been when he and his family had first arrived, by its grandeur. Brazier was no stranger to hotels – they were an occupational hazard for project managing IT consultants – but this one was a bit special. Not for the first time, he wondered if they had over-reached themselves financially somewhat by staying here, but Tricia had been insistent; she had wanted to stay somewhere stylish to meet Colin's new wife. Still, at least the loyalty points had come in handy; Graham had blown his entire balance on this stay and at least that had helped to mitigate the financial impact.

Grand lobby or not, though, Graham's immediate priority was on more prosaic matters and he quickly located the gents' and headed there. On the way, he passed an Oriental hotel manager, scurrying out of the restaurant at a brisk canter. The little man wore a crisp black suit, silver glasses and a very worried frown. He gave off an air of nervous efficiency as he passed, and Graham reflected that at least he wasn't the only one in the hotel feeling stressed at the moment.

Once out of the gents', Graham made a beeline for the bar. He found it around the corner from the main reception desk. It was sparsely populated at this time; glancing to his right, he saw a couple of smartly dressed businessmen in discussion; legs crossed, hands articulating, tall glasses on the table between them. To the left, a large black man and a thinner, grey-haired white companion sat drinking beer in easy chairs. Graham caught the tone of American accents.

There was one other man at the bar, sitting on a stool at the far end, head down, reading a broadsheet newspaper. He might as well have had a "Do Not Disturb" sign over his head. Graham nodded to the bartender.

"Good evening, sir. How are you?" asked the barman in excellent but slightly accented English.

Graham clocked the silver badge on his white shirt: Oleksanders. An Eastern European name – Latvian? Ukrainian? Probably somewhere around there.

"I'm, er... yeah, not too bad thanks," he said, deciding to keep his burdens to himself.

"What can I get you?"

Graham surveyed the draught lagers, pointed to one and said, "I'll take a pint of that please."

"No problem, sir. How are you enjoying your stay?"

"It's a great hotel, really nice. Lovely city, too."

"Yes, it is a very beautiful city, but it gets very hot this time of year, yes?"

Graham agreed as he signed for the drink, and then settled himself onto the barstool. He took a sip of his lager and took a moment to savour the cool liquid, letting the bubbles collect and pop on his tongue.

Oleksanders was busying himself drying glasses with a towel.

"How long have you been here? I haven't seen you in here before."

"We arrived quite late last night. This is our first full day, but we're here in the hotel for a week. It's part of a longer three week trip."

"Very nice."

"I think we might have overdone it a bit today, though" said Graham, as he took a second pull at the beer.

"Oh?" Oleksanders looked quizzical.

"I think we may have tried to do a bit too much. We walked right across the city. Under-estimated the heat and humidity. The jet lag too, probably. My step-daughter got a bit tired." *Well, that was a euphemism, if ever there was one*, he thought. "She's fourteen," he added as if by way of explanation.

Oleksanders smiled and continued with his drying. "Difficult age, yes?"

Graham arched his eyebrows and took another drink.

"How about you? How do you find yourself in this part of the world? You're a long way from home, aren't you?"

Oleksanders carefully placed the dried glass onto a shelf. "So, I have been here two months now. I have daughter too, but she is only eight. She's back home in Kiev with my wife. This is what I do – hotel bars, cruise ships. I will work here for six, maybe seven months, and then go home. Then, next year, same thing."

"Sounds like a tough life. You must miss them," said Graham.

The barman's smile faltered. "Yes, I do," he said quietly. "We call, Skype, but it is difficult. I usually cry." He gave Graham a little grin, but the Englishman thought it more of a grimace.

Oleksanders brightened, "But the pay is good, and it is a great city, so... not so bad."

The man from the tourist couple sauntered up to the bar and ordered two gin and tonics. Oleksanders busied himself with the drinks and Graham sipped his beer and wondered whether Gaby had come out of the bathroom yet. She had probably come out as soon as I left, he thought. He just didn't seem to be able to get through to her. He felt that she'd never liked him, right from the off. It wasn't his fault that her parents had split up before he'd even met Tricia, but that didn't stop Gaby from seeming to think that he had been the culprit who'd finished it all. He'd tried, of course – again and again. He'd spent time with her, bought her presents, given her space, but none of it had seemed to work. Maybe they were just destined never to get on.

He finished the last of his beer and replaced the glass on the bar. Oleksanders looked up with a smile, "Another one?"

"Not just now thanks, I've just remembered there was something I needed to do," said Graham, fishing out his pack of cigarettes and heading outside the main doors to join the other smokers.

When Graham returned to their room, Tricia was still asleep, but Gaby was lying on her back on the sofa, showered and wearing one of the hotel's fluffy white robes. She was wearing her ear buds and held her mobile at arms' length in front of her face, smiling as her thumbs worked the phone's screen.

She looks in a better mood, thought Graham, and he offered her a conciliatory "Hi." There was no response, but that was preferable to a slanging match, so he was happy to take it. Graham made his wife a cup of tea, and took it across to her, gently shaking her awake. She smiled when she saw the tea and then glanced over at her daughter, and seeing Gaby happily engaged with her phone, she smiled again.

"Thanks, darling."

Tricia propped herself up on her pillows. She inclined her head towards Gaby and gave Graham a surreptitious thumbs up.

Graham responded by waggling his horizontal hand noncommittally and shrugged his shoulders.

Graham sat down on the edge of the bed. "I'm sorry about earlier. I just… got a bit stressed."

"I know, sweetheart, I know. It's OK. What time is it?"

"Just gone 5.30pm. We should think about starting to get ready."

Tricia looked slightly pained. "I'm not really sure I'm in the mood for a restaurant, love" she said.

"Oh, really?" Graham tried to hide his disappointment; he'd been looking forward to a nice evening in the hotel's restaurant.

"I'm so tired, Graham. I'm not really sure I can be bothered. But if you…"

"No, no, it's fine, honestly."

"Honestly?"

"Yes, honestly. Look, we'll get some room service, order a bottle of wine. It'll be nice, we can sit out on the balcony afterwards."

Tricia leaned back against her pillow and breathed out. "Oh thanks, Darling. It'll be lovely, just the three of us."

Graham glanced across at Gaby who still lay on her bed, totally engrossed in her phone.

"Yes," he said, "It will."

Flight Crew

Captain Rob Mitchell had flown this flightpath many times before, mainly, as now, in the early morning thanks to the timing of the flight from London. As well as having flown it for real, it was also a bit of a simulator classic so he was very well versed in this particular approach. He arched his back, stretched his arms out in front of him, clasped his hands and managed to get a satisfying click from his fingers. The First Officer looked across at him, "Long flight, huh?"

Rob grunted assent and looked out of his window on the left-hand side of the aircraft. 5,000 feet below, the sunrise was casting the islets of the city's greater harbour in a warm salmon glow; the light bounced tantalisingly off the ocean's small chop. He usually enjoyed this part of the approach; after flying through the night and enduring an expanse of darkness across central Asia, only illuminated by the occasional thunderstorm, sunbeams on the ocean were always welcome.

His musings were interrupted by Air Traffic Control:

"CF54, you are cleared for landing on Runway two-seven."

"Roger, CF54 cleared for two-seven," Rob replied.

The First Officer moved the control column to align to the correct heading and then asked the cabin crew to prepare for landing.

The big plane dropped lower, its engines spooling back as it eased towards the runway.

The First Officer moved the throttle back marginally, to keep aligned with the Instrument Landing System.

Rob flicked his eyes across the instruments and onto the First Officer. Happy that she was flying the aircraft to his satisfaction, he resumed his musing. Normally, this view lifted his heart and left him yearning to be let loose in the city but this time, he just felt numb. At least he'd be staying in his favourite hotel, though, he thought; his mood lifted a little at the thought.

To his right, Sarah Booth was making her final corrections to ensure that the Airbus was aligned with the runway. The plane crossed the airport's perimeter; short, cropped grass passing under the wings. Gently caressing the control column to finesse the landing, Sarah floated the plane just above the runway as it lost its final few metres of altitude. Beneath them, the black and white stripes of the runway threshold flashed by and then the main gear made gentle contact with the ground, and they were down. Carefully, Sarah brought the nose gear down, slowed the aircraft and pulled off the runway, taxiing towards the terminal buildings.

"Missed the threshold," muttered Rob.

Sarah looked across at him for a moment, keeping her eyes locked on him for a fraction longer than was necessary. She knew that her landing had been nigh-on perfect but she'd flown with Rob before and had realised several flights ago that he liked to criticise – and usually not constructively. With a barely perceptible shake of her head, she moved her gaze back to the windshield and the approaching gate.

*

Half an hour later, the crew were walking through the Arrivals Hall, wheeling their trollies behind them. Dana always hated this bit. At the end of the flight, she just wanted to be able to be transported directly to her hotel, where a quick nap would usually precede an indulgent bath and then an afternoon of sunbathing around the pool. What she absolutely didn't need at this point was to have to stand in line at passport control, even if the crew did get to jump past the main queue of weary passengers. Some of them now turned and gave a slight half smile as she and the rest of the flight crew moved past them to the front of the line. From others, she heard some of the inevitable tutting as they realised they had been de-prioritised. Well, screw them, she thought. She'd been nice to these folks for over ten hours on the flight, and she didn't have to be any more. Standing behind the other flight attendants, she briefly perused her nails before being summoned forward to the desk. Handing over her US passport to a stocky, balding immigration officer, she let her mind wander again to the prospect of that long-awaited nap.

Passport returned, Dana wheeled her flight case through the immigration channel and gathered together with her colleagues, as they waited for the remainder of the crew to pass through. As usual, Rob Mitchell took charge, ushering the small group out towards the waiting minibus and issuing instructions in his precise, clipped, English accent. Dana enjoyed being with her British colleagues; for the most part, they were professional and good fun in equal measure but, even after five years, she still found herself marvelling on occasion at what seemed to her to be their cut-glass accents.

Emerging from the air-conditioned airport building out into the open, she was assaulted by both a wave of humidity and a glaring brightness which had her reaching into her bag for her sunglasses. Dana slipped the shades on and briefly ran her hand through her dark, glossy hair as she waited to climb into the minibus. Inside, she found herself sitting squeezed in next to Mitchell. She felt their thighs touching, separated only by the thinness of their clothing, and her mind drifted back to a night not so long ago, on the other side of the world, when she and Rob had… well, maybe that was best forgotten. She shifted position, crossed one leg over the other and smoothed her skirt. Beside her, Mitchell was looking out of his window as the minibus pulled out of the airport and onto the highway. Ignoring me, she wondered, or is he thinking of that night too?

The minibus picked up speed as it moved onto the free-flowing highway and towards the centre of the city. Dana caught sight of the driver looking at her through the rear-view mirror. Quickly, the driver returned his attention to the road and Dana smiled to herself. You've still got it, Babe, she thought, even after a ten-hour flight and feeling like shit. Now staring ahead as he drove, the driver addressed the passengers in general, "You hear about the protests?"

The crew mumbled assent. Sarah Booth looked up. "How bad are they?"

"Ah, not so bad. Mainly just in the east of the city, in one of the parks. Mostly, you don't see anything over this side."

"It looked pretty bad on TV," said Rob.

"There has been some violence, but just in that area," answered the driver.

"Have you seen any of it?" asked one of the stewards.

"Only a little. There was a big protest last weekend. Lots of people went; I went along too, just to see what was going on."

"And what was?"

"Well, it was mainly peaceful, but there were a lot of police around. A lot. There was lots of chanting. I heard later there was some trouble, but I didn't see anything."

As the questions flowed, Dana let the conversation wash over her and instead gazed out of her window. The minibus was slowing down now as it hit traffic on the edge of the city centre. Above them, residential tower blocks soared skyward, many of the windows bearing racks of clothes, doing their best to dry in the humidity. Dana always wondered what state the clothes would be in when their owners finally hauled them back inside. Dry, for sure, but probably also tainted with the fumes from the traffic. She pulled her gaze back to ground level; the tower blocks always made her feel a little claustrophobic, and the cramped confines of the minibus didn't help either. She really, really needed that nap.

The Manager

Behind the imposing oak door of the manager's office, Mr Lee Chung hung up the phone and scowled. He leaned back in his leather chair, rubbed his forehead and closed his eyes. He could feel a headache coming on; a big one. Yet another staff member had called in sick. It meant that cover in the restaurant tonight was going to be very limited, and that meant increased waiting time for guests, and that meant complaints. And those, he could well do without; he had enough to worry about with the tower renovations running behind schedule. Damn those protests, he thought. For he was sure that was the reason that so many of his employees wouldn't be working tonight; either too afraid to try to negotiate their way through the protests when coming from the eastern part of the city or, more likely, taking part in them. Greater democracy and increased freedom of speech were all very well, he thought, but did it have to interfere with the smooth running of his beloved hotel?

He slowly opened his eyes again and let his vision refocus. On the wall at the far end of his spacious office hung a map of the city. He got up from his chair and wandered over to it, brushing a few specks from the sleeve of his otherwise immaculate black suit jacket. Studying the map, he let his eyes wander over the layout of the city, from the harbour, with its bridges and pontoons, down towards where the hotel was situated, at the southerly edge of the prime downtown real estate. Looking across to the east of the map, he saw the large expanse of greenery which marked the city's largest park, and site of most of the protests, and, beyond that, the tightly packed residential tenement areas which had supplied most of the protesters. Right at the bottom of the map, the International Airport just managed to squeeze into view. He sighed and then, with a sudden renewal of purpose, he turned around and headed out of his office.

As he walked through the lobby, a passing bell boy noticed him and greeted him deferentially. Mr Chung nodded back in reply and carried on walking towards the restaurant. An airline flight crew was just on their way in through the main doors, and other hotel guests were dotted throughout the large space. Everything felt normal to Mr Chung; a casual observer wouldn't realise that there were protests of any kind going on in the city. He really wished there weren't;

it would make his life an awful lot easier. But, still, the reality was that they were taking place, he was going to be short staffed, and he needed to do something about it.

The restaurant was sparsely populated. Only a few of the white-clothed tables were occupied, with the last of the breakfast guests finishing their meals. Staff were already clearing away and starting to make their preparations for lunch. As he entered the restaurant, he nodded a greeting to two guests who were just leaving, a large, heavy-set black man and his colleague, a wiry white man, who had gelled his silver hair so that it swept back dramatically from a widow's peak. As they passed him, Mr Chung caught the distinctive twang of American accents. Heading into the restaurant's tiny office, he found its manager at his computer.

The restaurant manager looked up from his computer screen and caught sight of Lee Chung's grave expression.

"Something up, Boss?" he asked in heavily accented English.

"Staff," said Mr Chung, "We have had three more call in to say they won't be working tonight. We will be very stretched."

The restaurant manager whistled through his teeth. "Three. Man, that's bad."

Mr Chung rhymed off the names who would now not be making their presence felt in the restaurant tonight. They would be down by two waiters and a bartender in addition to the other catering staff who had already called in.

The manager pulled out his staffing plan and began to make crossings-out on it, whilst also re-positioning some of the remaining names. Mr Chung looked on approvingly; the protests might be causing him some unease, but he had faith that his staff would be able to deal with any issues which they caused.

The Envelope

As he took off his jacket, he could feel the bulk of the envelope in the inside pocket. Rob Mitchell carefully hung the jacket on a coat hanger and placed it in the wardrobe. He left the envelope where it was. He didn't want to think about it or its contents right now; there'd be time enough for that in the days and weeks ahead. But, even so, that little bulge in the inside pocket sent a little frisson of tension across his skin. He closed the wardrobe door and wandered over to the mini bar. He opened it, selected a whisky and settled down in one of his room's comfortable armchairs. Flipping on the TV with the remote he started to surf the channels. There were two types of pilot on long-haul flights – those who arrived, went straight to bed and tried, often in vain, to go to sleep. And then there were those, like him, who had just finished their working day and wanted to relax a bit. If he worked a more mundane job, the likelihood was that he would get home, grab himself a drink and watch a bit of TV. So why should it be any different for him, even if he was on the other side of the world from where he'd started his working day? And even if it was 10am?

He took a slug of the whisky and changed to the news channels. He flicked through a few of them... BBC, CNN, Sky, PNN. The same sorts of stories on most of them – US mid-terms, tension in the Middle East, Brexit shit from back home. Christ, when were they going to get that sorted? The sooner the better as far as he was concerned. One channel was showing the protests in the city, and he lingered for a few seconds, but then moved on to something more interesting. The protests had been going on for weeks now, and hardly anything had happened. Still, that hadn't stopped Tabitha and Megan worrying about him, and pleading with him not to go. He smiled as he thought about his daughters, but then the smile faded as he thought about the envelope lurking in his jacket pocket.

He swigged back the last of his whisky and then pulled another from the mini bar. He relished the fiery sensation as he swallowed it, and he returned his attention to the TV screen. Another couple of drinks and then he would hit the sack. His eyes felt gritty and raw, but he knew that if he went straight to bed, then sleep would elude him.

As the mid-morning sun streamed into his room, he sat there, drinking steadily and staring at the TV.

Dana

There was a loud shrill as the phone's alarm went off, and, after a few seconds, Dana reached out a groggy arm to grope for it. Her hand moved around on the bedside table but to no avail. Eventually, and reluctantly, she forced her head off the pillow, pulled up the eye mask which she had been wearing and finally managed to switch off the alarm. For a moment, she allowed her head to drop back onto the pillow as she gathered her thoughts. Don't go back to sleep, she told herself. She'd made that mistake before when flying long-haul and that sure was a great way to screw up your body clock during a three-day stopover. Forcing yourself to wake up in the middle of the day was the only way to deal with the jetlag but experience didn't make it any easier to deal with.

Summoning what seemed like almost all of her willpower, she managed to prop herself up on her elbow and, with the other hand, pulled the eye mask back over her head. She let it drop onto the floor beside the bed and rubbed her eyes. She took a sip of water from the glass on the table beside her and then swung her legs over the side of the bed. For a moment, she sat there, feet just touching the floor, shoulders stooped, both palms flat against the mattress, her head hanging low, and her long hair even lower. Eventually, she eased herself off the bed and moved across to the window, where a laser-thin shaft of light was coming through the gap where the curtains didn't quite meet. Steeling herself, she moved one of the curtains back. Bright sunlight suddenly flooded the room, and she stepped back involuntarily, shielding her face.

As her eyes became accustomed to the light, she was able to take away her protective hand and open the other curtain. The room had a good view, with a vista taking in a decent portion of the harbour and the city beyond, the midday sun glinting off the skyscrapers which comprised its iconic skyline. Below her was a place more impressive to her than the skyline; the place that she had daydreamed about as she had stood in line at passport control - the pool. She stared down from her vantage point on the large square of turquoise. She could see people within it, some more or less stationary, others more mobile, and still others progressing at speed in straight lines up and down as they ploughed through the water like miniature Olympians. Around the pool, the sun loungers looked particularly inviting, and it was the sight of them that revitalised her as she headed for the bathroom.

She luxuriated in the steady, comforting drizzle of the shower, feeling her tiredness ebb away. She was sorry to have to get out but, as she towelled herself dry, the thought of whiling away the afternoon basking in the warm embrace of the sun brought an involuntary smile to her lips.

Now feeling as fresh as she ever did on day one of a long-haul stayover, she rooted through her flight case for a bikini, and also fished out the weighty blockbuster novel that she was reading. Dana pouted at herself in the mirror as she straightened her hair and smiled again. It was for afternoons like the one she had in prospect that made flying worthwhile. Bring it on, Baby, she thought to herself, bring it on…

Stress

Mr Chung closed the door of his office and, for a moment, leaned back against it, his arms clasped behind his back. He closed his eyes and took a deep breath; he made a conscious effort to exhale deeply. Lee Chung was a man who was in tune with his own body, and, he knew that normally, this small exercise would have helped to lift any burden of stress, but not this time. This evening, Mr Chung was experiencing a very high level of stress. He had initially been becalmed somewhat by talking to his restaurant manager about the staffing situation. His manager was a good man, and Lee knew that he would manage the situation in the restaurant well tonight, but what he had just heard from an employee worried him. Worried him deeply.

He switched on the TV which was an omnipresent if slightly odd fixture on his mahogany desk. He didn't feel like sitting down, so he paced nervously for the few seconds it took for the television to come to life. He quickly flicked to a news channel and, sure enough, the channel was reporting on the protests in the park. His eyes darted back to his wall-mounted map of the city and lingered for a moment on that green expanse on the eastern fringes. Then his gaze returned to the live scene playing out on the TV; there was little greenery on view there, even though the footage was of exactly the same part of the city. Instead, there was what looked like a crowd on the edge. Protesters seemed to be whipping themselves up into a sort of hysteria; there was angry chanting, and some of the protesters were now wearing masks or scarves over their faces. The police were maintaining a solid line, but the line looked shaky and infirm as the crowd seemed to surge in rhythmic pulses, pushing up against and testing that sliver of authority.

Lee Chung was sure that in the next hour or so, this situation was going to get worse, possibly much worse. The member of staff he had just spoken to was going off shift and was heading directly to the park. Moreover, she had told him that she was doing so because she was responding to messages which had been sent directly to sympathisers of the protest movement, and that she was likely to be joined there by, literally, thousands of others.

Chung's earlier worries about staffing now seemed trivial and trite. What concerned him now was whether anarchy was about to break out in his beloved city.

Poolside

Dana felt horny. She put down her monstrously sized novel, propped herself up on her sun lounger and took a sip of her cocktail. She luxuriated for a moment in the warm wash of the sun and then, peeking over the top of her shades, took a look around the swimming pool area. She lowered her sunglasses a little more so she could get a better look at the other pool-goers. Not too much talent, she thought, but, hey, it's early... Sarah Booth walked past her line of sight, wearing a triathlete's swimming training costume. Dana gave the First Officer a little wiggle of her fingers as she passed, and Sarah smiled back before standing at the pool's edge and running through some stretching exercises.

Feeling horny was a fairly regular occurrence for Dana on long haul trips, and she usually did something about it. She dragged on the cocktail's straw once more and her mind wandered back to previous conquests on her various stayovers around the world. Layovers might be a better word for them, she thought. She chuckled to herself a little as she remembered that one, winced a little as she remembered that one, and felt herself reddening slightly as she thought about *that* one. Well, she thought, you can take the lady outta Lubbock but you sure as hell can't take Lubbock outta the lady. She snorted slightly with suppressed amusement as she thought that, and then reached down for her novel again.

Beyond, Sarah slipped into the pool – strictly obeying the "No diving" sign – and then commenced the first of many planned lengths of front crawl. Dana looked up and watched her for a moment. A pair of small children manoeuvred out of the way as Sarah arrowed her way past. Dana watched Sarah glide through the water, seemingly effortlessly, barely registering a ripple, let alone a splash, as she cruised down the length of the pool. Reaching the far end, Sarah executed a graceful and faultless tumble turn. Some woman, thought Dana. Pilot, triathlete and not yet even thirty. She gratifyingly took another sip of her cocktail as she watched the Englishwoman start her second length.

In the background, the sun glinted dazzlingly off the skyscrapers on the other side of the harbour. Seagulls wheeled overhead. Dana went back to reading her novel.

Her training session over, Sarah climbed out of the pool and stood for a moment as she let the sun start to dry her off. Her muscles felt lithe and warm and she felt content; she relished being able to unwind with some serious exercise after such a long flight. The flight. She thought back to those ten hours as she moved towards the sun lounger where she had left her towel. There was no doubt that Rob Mitchell was one of the best captains in the airline. He was also, she was sure, one of the grumpiest. She thought about his surly attitude, which had been on display for almost the entire flight and then, that moment, just after landing, when he had criticised her for missing the threshold of the runway. Had she missed the threshold? She didn't think so and, even if she had, it would have been by a matter of centimetres. She knew she'd flown a good approach and landing – especially given that it was her first into the city. The landing had been what she liked to think of as "driving onto the runway." That was what she called it when the plane touched down so gently that you barely noticed it. And Rob Mitchell had had the gall to criticise it. Still, she thought, that was his problem.

She towelled her hair with vigorous enthusiasm and looked around. Dana was gone. Sarah liked Dana, although they didn't have a lot in common. Sarah liked to keep busy on stopovers, maxing out her time so that she fit in her training regime, took in the local sights and culture and worked at night on building her knowledge of the Airbus. Dana was, well... Dana. Sarah had never seen her in a hotel gym, exploring a city or even in the swimming pool. What she had seen her doing plenty of was soaking up the sun *around* the pool and then spending lots of time in hotel bars afterwards. Ah well, each to their own.

She ordered herself a smoothie from the poolside bar and sat on the edge of a lounger whilst she drank it. Beyond the edge of the pool, the sun was continuing its journey westwards, moving now behind the towers of the city's financial district and starting to take on the reddish glow of late afternoon. She wondered about what she might do tomorrow and thought she might take in a couple of the museums. She always liked to get a feel for the history and culture of a place on her first trip there; she felt that it set the tone for any future trips and gave her some context to the location. Then her mind drifted to the protests that they'd been discussing in the taxi. She hoped they wouldn't interfere with her plans. After all, they *had* looked quite bad on the TV, but the taxi driver had reassured them that they looked worse than they actually were. She told herself that everything would be OK, but she wasn't entirely sure she had convinced herself.

Mitchell

Rob Mitchell awoke with a start and, for a moment, couldn't remember where he was. He raised his head and looked around. He was lying prone on a double bed, on top of the duvet. Hazy sunlight, the kind you get in the later afternoon, was flooding the room he was in, suffusing everything with a drowsy orange glow. Not ideal when you were trying to wake up. Over by the table that the TV sat on were several empty miniature whisky bottles. Two more lay on their sides on his bedside table. His head thumped, and he groaned. Then memories began to swim to the surface of his mind. The final approach – sunrise on the ocean below. That uptight goody two shoes bitch Sarah Booth sitting to his right, flying the aircraft. A minibus. A hotel. This hotel. He knew where he was. And he was hungover.

He clambered off the bed and went in search of water; his tongue felt thick and sticky. He found a glass, swilled water into it from his bathroom sink and gulped it down. Then he remembered the envelope and he felt a little burst of adrenaline. He tried to put the thought out of his mind and, instead, checked the time; coming up to 6.30pm. The rest of the crew would be assembling downstairs soon for pre-dinner drinks. As he stepped into the shower, he tried to remember who had been on the aircraft with him. Ryan – something. What was that guy's surname? It wouldn't come to him and he tried to think about who else was on the flight. Sarah Booth, as co-pilot, obviously. He still thought of them as co-pilots, not First Officers. He hated to admit it, she was a good pilot, but Christ she was dull. Then there was Rachel Bray – she was quite good fun. And Dana. He smiled involuntarily as he thought of her. Dana Weiss – it had been their first flight together since they had got it on last year. He rinsed his hair and wondered if it would be on the cards again tonight.

The Park

Across the city, in the verdant parkland that Mr Chung had just been perusing on his map, Steve Hannigan was preparing to record his piece to camera. He looked around him; behind him was a thick copse of trees, but on three sides, he seemed to be surrounded by a mass of humanity. The noise was incessant. Chanting and shouts of protest washed towards him, seemingly from all directions, although he knew that the protesters were all corralled in front of the trees. Police whistles sounded and, somewhere out in the crowd, drums were beating. As he gazed out, he tried to estimate the size of the crowd. Difficult, but he had been in these types of situation before, and he was pretty sure he'd be able to come up with a decent number that was at least halfway to the truth. Sure, Afghanistan and Somalia had been very different propositions, but both had involved huge crowds at different times, and he felt that he'd got himself a knack for understanding the size of a crowd. He cast his eyes over the sea of people again. At least a hundred thousand, he thought – possibly heading towards a hundred and fifty. No doubt the protesters would subsequently claim more, and the police and the city officials would claim fewer. He felt that his estimate would be somewhere in the middle, and about right.

"You ready, Steve?" asked Dave Geddes. Steve Hannigan knew that most news gathering organisations these days operated on something of a shoestring, but he was pretty sure that Planet News Network was more frugal than most. Whereas other broadcasters would have two or even three people supporting the broadcaster, PNN employed just one but, in Geddes, Hannigan knew that he had the best. He also compared Geddes' workload unfavourably with his own. Unfavourable, that is, from the point of view that it was Geddes catching the shit trip and he, Hannigan, who was getting off lightly. But then again, it wasn't Geddes who was the face of the news; it wasn't Geddes who was stopped in airports and mid-mouthful in restaurants to be assailed as "That guy from the TV" and asked for selfies and autographs.

"Steve?"

"Ah, sorry Dave," Hannigan came out of his reverie and snapped back into the current situation. "Yeah, just gimme a few…" he cleared his throat, cursorily wiped his forehead and once more flicked his eyes across the crowd.

"OK, ready when you are."

"You got it, Steve. OK, rolling in… three, two, one…"

Geddes nodded to Hannigan, who immediately switched on his camera persona; tight, clenched jaw, serious expression, hands held at chest height, ready to help explain the situation with helpful iterations for the watching public.

"Here, for the eighth day in a row, the crowds are massing, and they show no signs of dispersing. In fact, the numbers of protesters are growing and growing. I estimate that there are over one hundred thousand here today, in the city's main park, and that number may be a significant under-estimate. The protesters' demands remain, as they have been throughout this stand-off with the government, for greater democratic freedoms, for greater free speech, and for the release of political prisoners. The government here continues to maintain that it does not hold any political prisoners, and that all rights of free speech and democratic freedoms are maintained to all citizens. There has so far been very little violence today, or on any of the previous days of protests, but the tension in the air is undeniable, and there is a very large and obvious police presence. Neither side will accept what the other says, and neither side is likely to back down, so where these protests will go, and what will happen next is far from certain."

Hannigan left a pregnant pause, and then Geddes called "Cut!"

And then, less formally, "OK Steve, that's in the can."

"Great," said Hannigan, "How was I?"

"Pompous and full of shit."

"Fuck you, Geddes," said Hannigan with a smirk, and he flipped the bird at his cameraman to emphasise the point.

"Nah, that was good, man," said Geddes.

"Probably not gonna pull up any trees in Detroit, though," mused Hannigan wryly. "Ever wonder why we do this? Sometimes I don't think anyone in the States gives a goddamn shit about any of what we do."

Geddes said something, but his reply was lost in a sudden wave of high-volume chanting from the crowd.

Colin

Ten minutes to six. Colin hunched further over his computer screen and idly watched the stock market ticker for a minute or so. He checked his emails – none had come in since he last checked a couple of minutes ago. He flicked open a news website and briefly ran his eye over the headlines. Nothing he didn't already know. He checked his watch again. Still ten minutes to six. Or was it nine now? He really, really didn't feel like meeting Graham tonight. Graham and Tricia. And that bratty kid of hers.

It suited Colin to live on the other side of the world to his brother, only seeing each other once, maybe twice if they were unlucky, in a year. The stilted meetups, the polite conversation which nobody gave a shit about, the long, embarrassing silences. The daughter sulking in the corner, on her phone all the time. But, blood being thicker than water and all that, they kept making the effort. Kept meeting up. Kept going for appearances' sake.

And tonight was going to be bloody awful, he knew it. Tonight, they would be meeting Greta. He remembered back three years ago, when it was Tricia who was the new bride in the family. Now it was his turn to bring a new woman into the fold, and Graham and Tricia would make a show of fussing over her and being all welcoming, and then they'd find out that they didn't have a damned thing in common. And Tricia's kid probably wouldn't even get off her arse to say hello.

He stood up and wandered over to his office's panoramic window; beyond it, the sun was setting, painting the harbour and its attendant skyscrapers in a diffuse pink glow. Over to the east, he could see the city's main park. The trees were visible enough, but the rest of its usual greenery was subsumed beneath a mass of people. God, there were more protesters there tonight than he'd ever seen before; he was sure of it. Now there were a few lights in amongst the people in the park, as the daylight started to fade.

A police helicopter buzzed past, outside his window, heading towards the park. In the harbour beyond, a coastguard cutter lay lazily at anchor. Reluctantly, Colin turned back to his desk, took a swig of cold coffee, and buttoned down the sleeves of his shirt. He retrieved his suit jacket from the back of his chair and slipped it on with the assured air of a senior partner in the business.

He picked up his phone and called Greta.

"Hi, it's me. I'm on my way."

"OK." He heard her pause. "I… I am looking forward to tonight Colin."

"Really?"

"Really." She was no longer hesitant, but insistent now. Perhaps too insistent. "Really I am, Colin. I want to meet them."

He wasn't convinced that her sudden enthusiasm was genuine, and if she was laying it on to try to drum up his own - well, it wasn't working.

He turned and stared morosely out of the big picture window.

"I wouldn't get too excited," he said, "It is my brother we're talking about here."

"Oh, Colin, please cheer up! What's the worst that can happen?"

The worst already has happened, thought Colin – Graham and his family are in town.

Exit

The sky was darkening as Hannigan helped Geddes pack away the equipment. Although PNN might be a miserly employer, at least modern technology meant that there wasn't much for the two of them to carry.

"You sure we should be leaving?" asked Geddes. "Feels like this crowd's gettin' kinda hot."

"It's been like this before," said Hannigan dismissively. "You think they're building up to something, and that it's all gonna go apeshit, and then nothing happens and it's a big anticlimax."

Dave Geddes cast his eyes over the crowd. It seemed bigger than ever to him. It felt alive, pulsing, breathing, angry. "I guess," he said in doubtful tones.

"I'm tellin' ya, Dave – ain't nothin' gonna happen! Not tonight, at any rate. Let's get our sorry asses back to the hotel, get some chow and a few drinks. We're gonna be here for days, man, and we can't stay around the protests the whole time."

Geddes gave him a quizzical look.

Hannigan waved him away with a disdainful hand. "Listen, I thought things might have gone off last night. That was more tense than this; I thought it was on the edge, which it was. It seems to have calmed down a bit now."

Geddes weighed up Hannigan's words; it did make sense – the reporter had been here over a week, compared to Geddes' twenty-four hours. He shrugged.

"OK, Steve – you're the boss, I guess," The prospect of some creature comforts was suddenly appealing to Geddes. He and Hannigan had been based in the park, watching the protests build up, all day. His feet ached, his back ached, and he could sure use a shower. The humidity of the day was almost gone, but the air was still sticky and sweet, and his T-shirt was pretty much stuck to his back with his own sweat.

They made their way out of the park, pushing their way through the protesters and skirting around police. More than once, Geddes looked back. Something was different tonight, he was sure of it; he could feel it; smell it, almost. And he was almost never wrong.

But, then again, neither was Steve Hannigan.

Metro

The metro train was relatively quiet considering it was early evening. Colin and Greta easily found seats, and Greta spent most of the journey making full use of the wifi service; she would have preferred to have talked to Colin but her husband, who sat in melancholy silence, clearly wasn't in the mood. Colin alternately picked at his shirt sleeve and looked at his feet. Every now and then, Greta looked over at him, but he didn't return any of her glances and, each time, she returned to her phone.

The train stopped at brightly coloured station after brightly coloured station. In between examining his shirt cuffs and his feet, Colin realised that virtually nobody was getting on their train, which was heading towards the southern downtown area. His interest suddenly piqued, he thought back to the massing crowd in the city's eastern park which he had seen from his office and wondered whether the platforms for trains heading east were full.

"Greta," he nudged, "have you noticed anything?"

"Mmmmm? What's that" Greta mumbled as she looked up from her phone.

"What do you notice about this train?"

"Good wifi?"

"No, come on… there's nobody on it. At this time of night! I bet they're all going the other way."

"What, towards…"

"The park, yeah. I saw them from the office – there seemed to be a lot more this evening than there have been on previous days."

"But nothing will happen, will it?"

"I'm not so sure," mused Colin as he looked out of his window.

Further along the same train, two of the other passengers heading south were Steve Hannigan and Dave Geddes but, wrapped up in their discussions on their latest news piece, they failed to notice the emptiness of the train. For once, the journalists' instinct had deserted them both.

In the Bar

Sarah wandered into the bar and looked around. Two of the male flight attendants, Ryan and Nigel, were there, sitting on comfortable leather sofas, both drinking white wine. She ordered herself a mineral water and walked across to join them. Nigel was in full flow, explaining to Ryan how well his niece was doing at her grammar school.

"Aren't you just the proud uncle?" she smiled, shoehorning herself into the conversation.

"Oh, hi, Sarah. Well, yes, and with every right to be! She's doing so well. We're ever so proud of her." He beamed an avuncular smile and took a sip of his wine. "Do you have kids? Or nephews or nieces?"

Sarah shook her head, "No, it's just me and my cat. Do you want to see a photo?"

She clicked her mobile on, opened up the photos app and scrolled through the last ten or so photos that were on there. They were all of a black and white cat in various locations around Sarah's flat.

"Ah, gorgeous," said Ryan effusively, "What's her name?"

"*His* name," said Sarah. "People always assume cats are female, for some reason. But this is George – Gorgeous George," she grinned.

Ryan and Nigel both made appreciative noises.

"So, what have you guys got planned for the next couple of days?"

"I thought I'd take that hop on, hop off bus out to one of the beaches," said Ryan, "It's my third time here and I've never been – and it's the right weather for it."

"Sleeping and shopping for me," said Nigel.

"That's my kinda day you're talkin' about," came a lazy drawl from behind the sofas. Nigel half turned, but he already knew who it was from the voice. "Dana, come and join us."

"Oh, I intend to, honey. Be right back!"

They all looked across at their colleague as she strode to the bar, her lustrous dark hair falling halfway down the back of her elegant red dress. Sarah looked down at her own blouse and skirt and, not for the first time in Dana's presence, felt quite dowdy. She turned her attention back to the two flight attendants; in her peripheral vision, she could see Dana engaging the bartender in conversation. She tried to avert her eyes but found that she couldn't – it was compulsive viewing. Dana was leaning in towards the barman, no doubt turning on all her Texan charm. For goodness' sake, thought Sarah, all she was doing was ordering a drink, and at 7pm, too! Had the woman no shame? Actually, she knew the answer to that.

Sarah could have continued watching this little vignette, but the chemistry was interrupted by the arrival of Rob Mitchell, looking effortlessly casual in a short-sleeved shirt and khaki slacks, his jet black hair swept back and neatly gelled. He barged to the bar and positioned himself alongside Dana. That broke the spell for Sarah, and she took a sip of her water and tried to find her way back into the conversation with her crew mates. Within a minute or so, they had been joined by Rob and Dana. Rob looked sullen; Dana had a half smile playing around her mouth. The conversation died away as they sat down. Rob reached for his beer and drank deeply.

"Something we said?" asked Dana.

Family Reunion

Colin and Greta walked into the bar. It was one of the few in the city that he hadn't used at one time or another for a business meeting. A large black serving counter ran across the back of the bar, illuminated tastefully by carefully positioned soft spotlighting. Behind the counter stood a single immaculately dressed bartender, wearing a crisp white shirt and black waistcoat. He was gangly and thin, and was busy making conversation to a rather glamorous, olive-skinned woman in a red dress who was leaning forward purposefully towards him. Several plush sofas were in the middle of the bar area, and small, round high tables, each with a couple of stools, lined its periphery. A pleasant-looking young woman with a short blonde bob sat on one of the sofas, opposite a couple of men, chatting amiably to them. Colin quickly flicked his eyes around the bar; there was no sign of Graham and his family.

"Nice place," observed Greta.

"Mmmmm, Graham must have come into a bit of money," replied Colin.

They were just about to start towards the bar when a serious-looking man in shirt and slacks brushed past them and hurried straight to the counter, where he stood right next to the woman in red, almost but not quite touching her. He placed his forearms down territorially on the black marble slab in front of him, and the barman immediately broke off his conversation with the woman and looked up. Within seconds, he was serving the man, pouring him a large beer, and the woman had repositioned herself so that she was no longer leaning across the counter. Colin observed the scene with wry amusement; if that wasn't a display of alpha male jealousy, then he didn't know what was. Greta had also noticed what was happening, and she caught his gaze briefly; they exchanged a rare knowing smile.

As the man and woman took their drinks and went to join the blonde woman and two men on the sofa, Colin and Greta took their place at the bar's counter and ordered gin and tonics. They were just turning away from the bar, in search of a table, when Graham, Tricia and Gaby walked in. Tricia spotted Colin and his wife and made a little "Ah!" sound. She raised her eyebrows and her right hand in greeting at the same time. Colin replaced his drink on the bar and stepped towards Graham.

"You made it, then."

"Hi Colin,"

The brothers clasped hands, but there was no warmth in it. As if sensing that he needed to make more of a show of seeing Colin again, Graham belatedly clasped his younger brother's arm just below the shoulder, but it was an awkward gesture and the two men broke apart, self-consciously. Graham smoothed his palms down the front of his jeans.

Meanwhile, Greta and Tricia were meeting for the first time.

"Lovely to meet you, Greta." Tricia leaned in towards her new sister-in-law and gave her a peck on the cheek. As she moved away, Greta was trying to respond with an air kiss for Tricia on the other cheek.

"Oh, we're going continental, are we?" blushed Tricia, "Sorry, I forgot. Is that how they do it in Germany? I thought it was just France. Oh no, sorry – isn't it Switzerland that you are from?" She realised she was starting to babble, stopped talking and completed the kissing manoeuvre.

"It's OK," laughed Greta, "Yes, I am Swiss. And it's lovely to meet you, too."

"Welcome to the family, Greta," said Graham, carefully completing the air kissing ballet with a deftness his wife had lacked.

"Thank you, Graham, and this… this must be Gaby." Greta looked towards the girl, who stood on the edge of the group, phone in hand, chewing gum. Gaby hesitated for a moment, then offered her hand with studied reluctance, and Greta shook it. "And wonderful to meet you, Gaby."

"Hello," said Gaby with a curt finality that cut off further discussion.

The group stood in an awkward silence for a few seconds.

"Well, we've just got drinks," said Colin, "What'll you all have?"

Flashpoint

It was as the collective Brazier clan was sitting down and trying to think of a conversation starter that, in the great park on the eastern side of the city, the first shots were fired. The mood at the protest rally had been growing steadily uglier. Protesters were hemmed in by the police, and more were arriving by the minute, joining the back of the crowd and pushing those in front of them forwards. A crush started to build, and some scuffles broke out within the heaving mass as it slowly inched forward en masse, like a stream of lava, thick and relentless. Feet were trodden on, arms were pinned, some people slipped. Caps and spectacles were dropped as the pressure built. People were piling up against each other, faces pressed into the backs of heads, torsos squeezed for air. A pungency of stale body odour emanated from within the crowd.

As the last, golden rays of evening yielded to the clutch of night, the people at the front of the crowd were under enormous pressure, squashed from behind, held back at the front by a mixture of police lines and temporary, waist-high barriers. Scores of activists found their thighs mashed against the barriers, unable to move any further forward. There were cries of pain as midriffs were crushed mercilessly. The cacophonous noises from the throng behind the barriers started to turn from a chorus of jeers and shouts to a low, discordant, moan. Then the screaming started.

On the other side of the barriers, the police, many of them young, raw, recruits, looked terrified. They linked arms and tried to face into the crush of protesters, but the pressure built. The screaming intensified, and some of the officers were spat at. With arms locked in with colleagues and no way to wipe them away, the gobbets of saliva remained on faces for several seconds, taking their time to viscously drop away to the floor.

Behind this front rank of officers, the police commanders were also becoming increasingly agitated. Orders were shouted to the crowd through megaphones, but to no effect; the hysteria was building and building. Something was thrown from within the crowd; a rock. It arced through the air, across the initial police line and struck one of the officers who was using a megaphone square in the forehead. He dropped the megaphone and staggered backwards, clutching desperately at his head, and trying to staunch the blood that was now pouring from it. The police officer to his left dropped his megaphone and went to his aid; the one to his right screamed fiercely but impotently at the crowd through his megaphone. More missiles started to fly from out of the crowd. The surging of the crowd intensified, as did the screams.

Overhead, a police helicopter hovered, a searchlight suspended beneath it now fully illuminated and focused on the front line of the crowd. Another police officer was struck, and then one of the barriers gave way. The line of police behind it collapsed as bodies flowed out of the crowd, a pressure-point finally lanced. Officers were trampled and protesters went sprawling as they fell through the gap and into the open space beyond. Hands, fingers, heads were all crushed. The helicopter's searchlight picked out the bright crimson of spilt blood.

"Back, back!" barked an officer desperately into his megaphone, but it was too late. The surge in the crowd turned to a flood, and more barriers gave way. More police went down under the wave of bodies falling forwards.

A young officer just behind the frontline snatched his firearm from its side holster and fired a couple of warning shots into the night air but he was almost immediately wrestled to the ground by a bulky activist tumbling through the breach in the barriers. The gun went off again as the two rolled on the floor, and blood oozed between the pair, as the young policeman first screamed and then lay still. A second policeman pulled out his pistol and shot squarely into the back of the protester. There were high pitched screams, and some of the crowd in the vicinity, terrified like trapped animals, tried to push back to where they had come from; the police officer loosed off a couple of shots after them, and two people fell. Now other protesters, seeing what was happening, rushed the officer and manhandled him to the floor. Hands clawed at him from multiple directions; blood ran, and chunks of the officer's hair were torn loose. His screams as he fell under the weight of the mob were terrible, but short-lived.

More shots rang out from across the park.

In the police helicopter, the crew looked down helplessly at the unfolding carnage beneath them. The pilot transmitted a curt radio message. It was a message which had been expected at some point, so the recipients were prepared and ready for it. On the edge of the city, the army began to mobilise.

<u>Mary</u>

Hannigan and Geddes clinked their beer bottles together and took simultaneous gulps

"That's better," said Hannigan, with satisfaction, wiping his mouth with the back of his hand.

"Sure was ready for that," agreed Geddes, "Bitch of a day."

"Yeah, it was a hot one, alright."

"Just gotta hit the men's room," said Geddes, sliding off his stool. "Back in a sec."

Hannigan took a further swig and replaced his bottle on the high table they were sitting at. Behind him, a group of men and women were drinking and chatting, a little too loudly, if truth be told. He let himself tune in to their conversation. Mainly English accents, but then he did pick out a fellow American. He turned slightly and saw that the rich brogue belonged to an attractive dark-haired woman in a red dress. She caught his glance, and he turned away, embarrassed that he had been caught looking. He took another mouthfeel of beer and, with the security of his back to the little group, tried to listen in again. He had a journalist's natural curiosity or, as Mary would put it, a talent for sticking his goddamn nose into other people's business. He caught the odd word floating up from the conversation at his back. "Roster, "flight pay", "Airbus". Flight crew, he thought.

Geddes re-joined him and took another pull of his beer.

"You and Mary been in touch since we got here?"

"Nah. We don't bother."

"What? Keepin' in touch?" Geddes shook his head ruefully, "Man, that's one easy-goin' wife you got there. Thought you'd need to be checkin' in with her."

Hannigan surveyed the label on his beer bottle, considering his words. Then he looked up and across at the older man. "It's not good, Dave. It's not been good for a while."

"Shit, sorry man, I didn't mean to…"

"It's OK. We're still with each other, but we're not really *with* each other, if you know what I mean. I do my thing, Mary does hers. My leaving DC didn't help."

Geddes nodded. "That's a shame. I always liked Mary."

Hannigan shrugged and supped his beer.

"It's the old story, I guess. We're pretty much still together for the sake of the kids. When they've all gone to college… well, we'll see. It's not gonna be long now. Greg's already at Keene State and Josh graduates high school next summer."

"And Lyndsy's what, fourteen, fifteen now?" asked Geddes.

"Fifteen," said Hannigan, "About her age." He nodded in the direction of a teenage girl sitting unhappily with four adults on the other side of the bar.

"But happier, I hope," said Dave Geddes with a chuckle.

"Oh yeah, you betcha. She's a good girl."

"Another?" Geddes gestured at Hannigan's empty beer bottle.

"What the fuck do you think?"

"I'll take that as a yes," laughed Geddes and ventured across to the bar.

TV News

Lee Chung returned to his office after dealing with a problem at the hotel's reception. He prided himself on the fact that he always seemed to be able to appease an irate guest; giving them his calm and undivided attention always seemed to do the trick. Tonight, though, he took no satisfaction from his latest triumph of diplomacy; the TV in his office, still tuned to the news channel, was showing horrific scenes in the park. Chaos seemed to have broken out there in the few minutes that he had been out of his office at reception. He stood transfixed by the ugly picture unfolding in front of him. A banner scrolled across the bottom of the screen, its simple message of "Riot breaks out at demonstration – shots fired into crowd. More to follow…" chilling to Mr Chung. "My god," he said out loud.

He bustled across to his desk, picked up his phone and called the hotel's head of security.

"Tony? Have you seen the news? It looks bad, very bad. There's rioting in the park. My office immediately please."

He replaced the phone in its cradle and drummed his fingers on the desk whilst he stared again at the TV. Then he picked up the phone and called his home. He spoke to his wife and started to explain the developing situation to her, but she had also been watching the news and was fully aware of what was going on. She reassured him that the children were with her, and that they would stay safely inside the apartment that evening. By the morning, she was sure, things would have calmed down, and the situation would be a lot clearer.

Chung hung up the phone. He just hoped that she was right.

Escalation

"Ah, hello again," Oleksanders greeted Graham Brazier as the Englishman approached the bar for drinks.

"Hi, er," Graham squinted at the bartender's name tag, "Oleksanders."

The barman smiled. "You meet your friends, yes?"

"It's my brother, actually. And his wife. His new wife, in fact. It's the first time we've met her. They live here."

"Ah, lovely. A family occasion – very nice."

"Yes, er... yes, it is." said Graham with little conviction.

The barman was too experienced and too professional to show he'd noticed Graham's lack of enthusiasm for the supposed lovely family occasion.

"We'll take another round of drinks, please."

"Of course, sir. Same again?"

"Yes please, and can we charge these to our room?"

"Yes. No problem."

Oleksanders busied himself behind the bar as Graham waited.

Suddenly, there was a sharp cry from behind him. "Oh!"

He turned around; a woman sitting with a man on the far side of the bar was looking aghast at her phone. "They're rioting!"

The casual conversation taking place across the bar ceased as though a switch had been thrown. There was quiet for a few seconds, then:

"What?"

"Where?"

"Here?"

The silence was broken as abruptly as it had descended. Mobile phones were pulled from pockets and lifted from tables. Abandoning the drinks, Graham rushed back across to the sofas that he and his family were occupying. Tricia and Colin were already thumbing their mobiles for updates, Greta was looking worried. Gaby, oblivious, sat slumped on the sofa, headphones in, head down, totally focused on her phone.

"What's going on?"

"Just trying to bring it up," said Colin.

Tricia got there first. "Look, here it is. Oh my god, it looks awful."

"What? What's happening?" asked Graham impatiently, manoeuvring to look over her shoulder.

"People have been shot – killed. Oh god, there's a huge riot going on, look."

Graham focused on the tiny screen. It showed flashes of gunfire and strobe lights against the stark blackness of the night sky.

From across the bar came a great shout, "Holy fuck!"

Instinctively, Graham looked across. The shouter was a big black guy, and he was also staring at his phone. As Graham watched, the man jumped off his bar stool. A thin, white man with silvery grey hair next to him also stood up from his stool, "I knew it, Steve, I knew it," Graham could hear the man saying.

In front of him, Gaby was slowly sensing that something was amiss. She removed one of her air buds and looked up from her phone questioningly, "What's happening, Mum?"

Tricia moved across and put her arm around her daughter. "I'm sure we'll be fine, darling, I'm sure we will."

"About what? About what, Mum? You're scaring me!"

"There's, well, there's a riot breaking out in another part of the city, but I'm sure we'll be fine here."

"A riot? What, like people fighting?"

"Gaby," said Colin, "Your mother's right. It's the other side of the city from here. The police will get it under control, I'm sure." But he didn't sound convinced. He glanced back down at his phone.

Across the bar, the black guy and his silver haired companion were hurrying out.

"Dave, get the camera and meet me in the lobby," Graham heard the black man shout as they disappeared out of the bar's entrance.

Behind his immaculate counter, Oleksanders was switching on the TV which was mounted on the wall alongside the rows of whisky and gin bottles. He quickly searched for a news channel and turned up the volume. The people in the bar started to congregate to watch.

The scrolling banner at the bottom of the screen now read, "Riots break out – many feared dead in pitched battles between police and protesters." Greta covered her mouth with her hand. Somebody murmured "Jesus H Christ" as the TV showed footage of police officers in full riot gear repeatedly beating protesters with short batons. The camera work was shaky and disjointed, as though the cameraman was ducking and dodging projectiles and people. Which he probably was, thought Graham Brazier as he looked on, with a sense of mounting anxiety.

Now the view on the TV switched to aerial footage, using night sights. The small crowd around the bar peered at the screen, trying to make out what the fuzzy green images were showing. A small line of indistinct dark green blobs seemed to be in transit along one of the main highways. Rob Mitchell was the first to work out what they were looking at.

"Jesus," he said, in a tone approaching awe, "those are tanks."

Into the Night

Dave Geddes charged out of the lift, camera in hand.

"Come on, man," urged Steve Hannigan.

"I knew we should never have left the park, I just knew it," panted Geddes.

"Yeah, OK, you made your point," snapped Hannigan, "Come on."

They rushed through the hotel's grand doors, which were hurriedly opened by a pair of startled concierges. Emerging out of the hotel's air-conditioned interior, the sticky, tropical night air was suddenly sultry and dangerous. Sirens – many sirens – could be heard in the distance as, could, ominously, the staccato cracks of pistol or rifle shots. A helicopter flew low overhead, green and red lights flashing alternately at its sides, the roar of its rotors reverberating madly off the skyscrapers that surrounded them.

"Metro!" shouted Hannigan to his colleague, and they set off towards the train station, half a kilometre or so from the hotel. There were people on the streets, but they were rushing to get off them, to get home, to find a place of safety. There was an air of barely subdued panic abroad; a second helicopter thudded low over them, but few looked up.

Hannigan and Geddes half jogged to the Metro station, Hannigan starting to sweat and pant as his bulk told against him. They reached the entrance, but it was blocked by a police officer, who stood firmly in their way.

"Gotta get a train," gasped Hannigan between laboured breaths.

"Closed," was the simple and unambiguous reply.

"Look, we've got to get to the park. We're press," said Geddes, "PNN?" he added hopefully.

"Closed," said the officer.

"Are there other stations that are open?"

"Closed."

"Ah fuck," said Hannigan, leaning against the wall of the station's entrance and breathing heavily. He wiped his forehead with a large white handkerchief.

"You leave now," said the police officer, making a go-away gesture to them.

"Taxi?" asked Geddes.

Hannigan nodded, and pushed himself off the wall. He and Geddes walked to the edge of the road. It was only then that they noticed that virtually all of the traffic was heading in one direction. There were virtually no cars going eastwards. They spotted a taxi and tried to hail it; it sped past. Another came, and then another. They tried on each occasion to flag the cab down, but both kept going.

"Ah, this is hopeless," lamented Hannigan.

"Let's go back to the hotel and see if we can borrow a car," suggested Geddes.

Hannigan nodded, "OK, good idea."

They set off, the lithe cameraman making the pace, his more heavyset colleague following at an increasing distance as they proceeded down the rapidly emptying streets.

Decisions

In the bar, Gaby was curled foetally on the sofa, her mother sitting next to her and stroking her shoulder. Tricia tried to comfort her daughter. Gaby had the frightened eyes of a cornered rabbit, and she was starting to hyperventilate.

"Mummy, I'm so scared, so scared…" she whimpered.

It was a struggle because of the way that Gaby was positioned on the sofa, but Tricia slid off the sofa into a kneeling position and tried to place both of her arms around Gaby's neck as her daughter quietly sobbed.

"Baby, it's going to be OK, it'll be OK, it will, it will," she soothed. Gaby continued to sob. Tricia rubbed her shoulder and looked over towards the TV screen.

It was the TV screen which was capturing the attention of everybody else in the bar. They stood in a little huddle in front of the bar's large counter, eyes glued to the screen, which was currently showing a mass of humanity streaming out of the park. "Rioters heading for downtown" the scrolling banner now read. Graham noticed that the former "protesters" and "demonstrators" were now "rioters" and wondered whether the government had intervened with the TV station. He thought back to some of the discussions he had had with Colin during their infrequent meetings over the last few years. He had wondered how Colin had felt, coming to live in a part of the world where the government was, well, if not totalitarian, at least authoritarian. Colin's response had been typical of a pragmatic financier; he just followed the money and, as long as the government didn't give him or his business any trouble – which they didn't – then that was fine with him. And to hell with human rights and democracy, Graham had thought at the time.

There was a tap on his shoulder. He half turned to see Colin standing behind him. Greta stood just behind Colin, her face pale and drawn. She held her hands in front of her face, steepled as though in prayer.

"Listen, I think it might be for the best if we think about heading home," he said to Graham, "Who knows where this might end up?"

Graham nodded. "Yes, of course, you should do that. Definitely."

An hour or so ago, the thought of the dysfunctional family reunion being cut so abruptly short would have filled him with joy; now, he didn't even register the fact that the evening was being drawn to a premature conclusion. His only thoughts were on what would happen next in this city, which suddenly seemed to have lost all sense of control.

The two men embraced, Graham rubbing his younger brother's back supportively and, as he did so, it occurred to him that they hadn't shown any sort of familiarity like this for years. Graham gave Greta a brisk hug, and then she and Colin moved across to the sofa to say hurried good-byes to Tricia and Gaby before hastening out of the bar.

The lobby had a strange, empty feel to it. The reception desks were abandoned, with the receptionists joining small huddles of people who were dotted throughout its large expanse, some looking at phones, others in earnest debate. Colin saw that the concierges had left their usual position by the doors and had gravitated towards the small knots of people. He saw the hotel manager, looking smart in his black suit, but like a man who had the worries of the world on his shoulders. The manager was in deep discussion with a large man in a suit which was far more crumpled and ill-fitting. The man in the crumpled suit was craning his neck downwards to catch what the manager was saying.

Colin grasped Greta's hand and they quickly walked over to the doors. Colin tried to push one of them open, only to find that it wouldn't budge. He tried the other door; that, too, was apparently locked. He stepped back, frustrated. Behind him came a voice, "Sir, sir?"

Colin looked around. The large man in the crumpled suit was approaching them. He had a lined face, a crew cut and a nose which looked like it had been broken several times. He limped slightly as he walked across. "Hello, sir. I'm Tony Johnson; I'm Head of Security for the hotel. I'm sorry but, under the circumstances, we have made the decision to lock the doors until the situation outside is clearer."

"But my wife and I need to get home."

"I understand, sir, but the safety of the guests and staff is of paramount importance to us. The doors are now locked."

"Look, Mr Johnson, I must insist…"

"I'm very sorry, sir, there is chaos on the streets, the army has been deployed and we have just heard that the metro system has been shut down. The decision is final."

Greta spoke up, "Please, we just want to get home. We're not guests here."

"I can't allow the doors to be opened. I really am very sorry." Johnson moved away, leaving Colin and Greta standing impotently in front of the doors.

"What are we going to do?" asked Greta.

"Well, we either look for another way to get out, or we're stuck here."

They both jumped as there was a sudden hammering on the other side of the doors. It was the large black guy and his silver haired companion who they had earlier seen in the bar.

"Hey, can you let us in?" the black man shouted. His voice was muffled by the great thickness of glass which stood between them.

"We're guests here," the silver haired man called.

Colin turned towards them, "They've locked the doors," he shouted, "They're not letting anyone in or out."

"What? Man, come on!" Steve Hannigan beat the flat of his palm on the glass.

"Hold on a sec," Colin shouted. He rushed off to find Tony Johnson and returned with him a few seconds later.

"We're guests," Hannigan and Geddes shouted in unison. "We need to get back in," added Geddes, somewhat unnecessarily.

Tony Johnson was a big man, bigger even than Hannigan, and he had a voice to match. "The doors are locked," he boomed, "For the safety of guests and staff. Entry and exit to the hotel is currently prohibited through the main doors. However, if we can verify that you are guests, we can allow you access back into the hotel through a rear door."

"We're journalists," shouted Hannigan, "PNN. We're not trying to get back into the hotel to stay there; we wanna see if we can borrow a car. We're trying to get to the protests. To film them."

Johnson appeared unmoved. "The situation is deteriorating all the time. The rioters are heading downtown. They are coming towards us."

On the other side of the glass, Hannigan and Geddes exchanged glances.

Hannigan turned back to the great door in front of him. "How far away are they?" he bellowed.

"A couple of kilometres, maybe less," Johnson shouted back.

Hannigan thought for a moment and then fished out his mobile. Colin watched through the door as the journalist tapped at his phone, the interior lights of the hotel's lobby shining off the sweat on the big man's forehead. Colin saw Hannigan turn to his colleague and say something, but he didn't catch what it was. Geddes hefted his camera. The two men turned and headed back out into the night.

Scenes on a TV

Dana nervously fingered the crucifix around her neck and bit her lower lip as she watched the TV. The scenes now were shot from a helicopter, and they showed total chaos in the streets. People were not just running down the main avenue of the city in a great tidal wave of humanity; they were fleeing. The resolution wasn't good enough to pick out individuals, but the overall impression was of the crowd acting as one, all heading in the same direction, panicked into a mass stampede.

There was a sudden, small, flare of orange light on the screen, followed by another.

"Petrol bomb," said somebody standing behind her.

"Jee-zus" breathed Dana, fiddling more intently with the crucifix. She looked around; all eyes were still glued to the screen; nobody was drinking anymore. She caught sight of a couple walking back into the bar. She recognised them as the people who had arrived at the same time as Rob Mitchell had muscled in on her conversation with the barman. The *cute* barman.

The man stopped in the entrance to the bar. The woman who was with him also stopped. Across the bar, a man sitting with a woman and a teenage girl who was curled up on the sofa looked up in surprise, "Colin!"

"Everybody, hey, everyone, excuse me, can I have your attention for a minute please?" called the man who had just come back into the bar.

Attention swung round from the TV to the man.

"I just wanted to let you know, because of the situation, they have locked the doors to the hotel. They aren't letting anyone in or out."

There was an audible gasp from those within the bar, and then some low level, muttered, but urgent, conversation amongst the various groups within the room.

Colin, along with Greta, made his way back across to his brother and his family.

"Guess we're stuck here for the duration then, huh?" asked Graham.

"Looking that way," said a tight-lipped Colin.

On the sofa, Gaby burst into tears. "I want to go home," she sobbed, "I don't want to be here. I just want to go home,"

"I know, Baby, I know," said Tricia, rocking her gently, as Greta looked on helplessly.

Graham walked back over to the TV and joined the small crowd standing there. More petrol bombs were being thrown. Smoke was now billowing from many different parts of the scene. Suddenly, the screen went blank and the assembled viewers groaned. Oleksanders fished out a remote control from behind his counter and tapped at it desperately as he pointed it towards the TV. He flicked from channel to channel, but there didn't appear to be anything being broadcast.

"The bastards; they've cut it!" Graham heard someone cry. In common with at least half of the people standing before the TV, he grabbed his mobile phone and tried to log onto the internet. Nothing.

"The internet's down, too... and I've got no phone signal. I had four bars a minute ago."

"Oh, bloody brilliant," shouted a man to his right in short-sleeved shirt and khaki slacks, "The city's going up in flames, and we haven't got a bloody clue now what's going on." His voice, though angry, was crisp and clipped. Unmistakably English.

There was a moment of silence, then a different voice said, "So now what do we do?"

Downtown

Hannigan and Geddes moved as swiftly as they could, weighed down both by the camera equipment and Hannigan's bulk. They were able to navigate their way easily enough onto the city's main thoroughfare. It was only a few hundred metres from the hotel and, once they were on it, they knew that all they had to do was point themselves eastward, in the direction of the park and head down the avenue. Pretty soon, they reckoned, they should encounter a swarm of people heading their way.

Steve Hannigan felt a familiar tingle of adrenaline as they moved down the street. This was nerve-wracking stuff, but it was what he lived for. It was basically what he had sacrificed his marriage and any semblance of a decent family life for. He had decided to make the foreign correspondent's brief his own over twenty years ago and it had put him into plenty of scrapes around the world; scrapes which he had always survived pretty much unscathed, save for a broken finger here or bout of food poisoning there. But there had always been one unifying theme of the trouble he had encountered in the past – almost without exception, it had taken place in some of the most godforsaken parts of the planet – Iraq, Libya, Afghanistan, the Central African Republic. This time, he was in one of the world's biggest metropolises and he was about to see it turn to rat-shit. This was big-time stuff, and he planned to be right in the middle of it; he was still kicking himself for not following Geddes' advice about staying put in the park, but now they could make amends. In fact, he thought, as they jog/walked down the street, things could have worked out for the best. Had they stayed in the park, chances were that they would have been able to film the start of the trouble, but would they have been able to get out with the crowd? He suspected they would have been pinned in the park, if not by the police, then just by the sheer volume of people, and they would have missed things really taking a turn for the worse. No, as he panted after his colleague, he was pretty sure that they were going to run headlong into a state of anarchy unfolding in front of them.

The road was brightly lit, with street lighting and the lights from shop windows illuminating the way. Eerily, there was no traffic, and they saw virtually nobody else on the street. As he jogged along, Hannigan thought that the police must have sealed off the road or must have held back all traffic at a certain point in the city. The citizens, he thought, must have done one of two things: joined the riot or fled.

Ahead, he could hear the noise of the riot – if that's what it was. He found himself wondering how he would describe it in his piece to camera in a few minutes' time. A riot? A demonstration? A government massacre? He had no doubt that there'd be violence and appalling brutality on both sides; there always was, it was just a case of calling it how you saw it. *Stay objective, stick to the facts, describe what you see.* The mantra of his first news editor swam through his mind like an annoying earworm from the radio which you couldn't shake off.

A few blocks further down, he could see smoke rising from behind the skyscrapers. The growing smog was illuminated by irregular flashes. He could now hear gunfire, too. Alarmingly, the sound of automatic fire was now mixed in with the echoing cracks of the pistol and rifle shots he'd heard earlier.

The first people in the wave of demonstrators (or were they rioters?) started to run past him and Geddes, like the advance shockwave of a turbulent current. He had a real sense of running against the flow of the tide and saw Geddes turn his head to look back at him. He was clearly sensing the same thing.

Hannigan signalled to his colleague to stop, and Geddes did so. Hannigan put his hands on his knees, bent double and breathed deeply, but the sticky tropical air burned hot and hard in his lungs and he panted for several seconds. He hawked up a gobbet of saliva and spat onto the pavement.

"You OK, Steve?" Dave Geddes asked. He didn't seem remotely physically troubled, despite just having jogged over a kilometre with a TV camera.

Hannigan, still bent double, held up a hand. After a few seconds, he straightened up, still gasping for air. Sweat was pouring off his forehead.

"Yeah, just… hold on."

He sucked in more air and seemed to regain some composure. More protesters ran past the two of them. Chaotic sounds swirled in the night air, seeming very close; screaming, shouting, sirens. Another helicopter passed overhead, very low, sweeping a searchlight from side to side as it went past.

"Let's… let's start filming. We're gettin' close now, real close. Start the camera, Dave."

Hannigan coughed up another ball of saliva.

"OK, game faces on," he said with grim determination.

Debate

The man in the short-sleeved shirt and khaki slacks cleared his throat.

"The best thing we can do is all stay calm and stay put."

"Shouldn't we go back to our rooms?" asked Tricia.

"I don't think so," said the man, "We've got no idea what's going on out there now, so we're better off sticking together. And don't forget – they've knocked out the TV, the internet and the phone signal. The electricity might be next and I, for one, don't want to be stuck in my room when that happens."

A few people within the bar assented, but Colin spoke up. "And you are?"

"My name's Rob. Rob Mitchell. I'm an airline captain; we flew in this morning. I know the city pretty well; I've been here many times."

"And I know it pretty well too. I've lived here for eleven years."

The two men assessed each other for a moment.

"Great," said Mitchell after an uncomfortably long pause, "that's good to know."

Graham Brazier spoke up. "We should probably look to see what's happening in the rest of the hotel. There isn't much point staying in here if there aren't going to be any updates."

There was a murmur of assent; Oleksanders came out from behind his bar counter and joined the guests. The eleven of them headed out of the bar, Tricia and Gaby trailing along behind Tricia with a supportive arm around her daughter, who had stopped crying but looked extremely pale.

The lobby was as it had been a few minutes earlier when Colin and Greta had tried to leave small groups of staff members, standing around in discussion. Now, though, there were no mobile phones to distract attention and the buzz of conversation in the room had a sharp worried, edge to it.

Lee Chung was in deep conversation with Tony Johnson when he spotted the guests filing out of the bar area. He waved them over towards him, and they obediently moved across.

"Good evening, I am Mr Lee Chung, the manager of the hotel, and this is our Head of Security Mr Tony Johnson." Johnson nodded towards them. "Obviously, we are tonight confronted by an unprecedented security situation. The serious rioting that has broken out in the city mean that we have had to lock the doors to the hotel. There is currently no access in or out. We ask you all to please remain calm. You will be safe here."

"You can't know that," said a guest who had come with a number of others from the restaurant.

"No, we don't know that for sure," admitted Chung, "but considering what is going on, this is the safest place to be right now."

Tony Johnson nodded agreement.

"What do you suggest we do now?" Greta asked Mr Chung.

Rob Mitchell interrupted, "It's like I said back there, we just have to sit tight. Hunker down here, wait it out."

"This gentleman is right," said Mr Chung, "that's all we can do at the moment. I suggest that all of you who are here now head back to your rooms. We have staff going along the corridors at the minute, asking people to remain within their rooms."

"No, we won't be doing that," said Mitchell.

Chung turned to him, "I'm sorry?"

"We're staying here. We've already agreed that. The internet's been cut, the TV, phones. Who's to say that the electricity won't be next? No, sorry, Mr Chung, but we're safer down here."

Chung regarded him for a moment and then slightly bowed his head and, with excruciating politeness, said "As you wish, but we would – ah – *prefer* it if guests returned to their rooms. We must ensure that we do not get too many people gathering down here. There would be a safety issue with too many people crowded into the lobby, but hopefully the other guests will remain in their rooms. I suppose if you have already agreed, though…"

"I didn't agree," a voice came from the back of the group.

Rob Mitchell looked around, "What?"

"I didn't agree to stay down here," said Dana.

"You did, back there. We just agreed it," said Mitchell.

"No, you told us. You told us we were staying down here – there was no discussion."

"Dana, I think you'll find that…"

"What, that you're the captain of the aircraft? I know that, Rob, but look around you, for Christsakes. This ain't no airplane – this is a hotel, baby."

Sarah Booth made a slight fist in front of her mouth and faked a cough to try to stifle the laugh that was trying to escape. In spite of the severity of the situation, she couldn't help but find this funny.

Mitchell sized up Dana for a moment and stood silently. Other than Sarah's cough, which seemed to echo off the marbled walls, there wasn't a sound, then, "OK, it's your choice of course. Do what you need to. Do what you think is best. All of you, do what you think best, but I'm staying down here."

I think we'd be better back in our room, Graham, don't you think?" asked Tricia, nodding her head towards Gaby, who looked stunned and tearful.

"Possibly," said Graham slowly. He clearly wasn't convinced, though. "I'm not sure I want to be cut off from what's going on…"

"Graham, we don't *know* what's going on!" Tricia cried, "It's a case of either hanging around down here and not knowing what's happening, or at least being in the safety of our room and not knowing. Either way, we're not going to know!"

Graham nodded as Colin spoke up, "Look, why don't you take Tricia and Gaby back to the room? I'll stay down here with Rob. If anything happens, I'll come and find you and let you know what's going on."

"And the electricity?" asked Graham.

"Well, it's on for now, and we don't know that it's going to go off. If it does, we'll just have to cross that bridge when we get to it, but I honestly think you'll be safer and more comfortable back in your room."

"You're probably right," said Graham.

They started to make their way towards the stairs, when Graham thought about Greta. He turned to his new sister-in-law, "What about you, Greta? Do you want to stay down here or do you want to come with us?"

Greta looked at Colin, who gave a slight nod.

"I'll come with you," she said, and followed towards the staircase, which Dana and the two stewards were already ascending.

Sarah Booth walked across to Rob, hoping that he hadn't noticed her involuntary giggle earlier. "I'll stay down here, Rob," she said, and then, turning to Colin, "Hi, I'm Sarah, I'm with the airline too."

"Colin Brazier." They shook hands, and Rob also offered his to Colin in something of a perfunctory gesture. Oleksanders wandered over to join them, and they stood in a loose semi-circle.

"So… not quite what I was expecting for this evening," said Sarah.

Colin gave a snort of laughter, "You can say that again. This was the night my brother and his family were meeting my wife for the first time. Now she's upstairs with them, and I'm down here waiting for who knows what…"

"I'm sure they'll be OK," said Sarah. "I'm sure we'll be OK. All of us."

"Are you?" asked Rob, "Because I'm not."

Reportage

Geddes started the camera and then counted Hannigan down to start his piece to camera. With years of experience behind him, Steve Hannigan was able to launch straight into his report, and talk off the cuff. Behind him, frightened citizens rushed past, their faces masks of panic; there was the sound of breaking glass and small explosions, very close now.

"The protesters have spilled out of the park, they have poured into the downtown area, and they seem to be fleeing. The army has been called in – they have been on high alert for days – and tanks have been mobilised." He paused and looked over his shoulder, then turned back to face the camera as more demonstrators raced past behind him. "This seems to be the front wave of what now appears to have turned into a mass riot. The main body of protesters, rioters – call them what you will – is just beyond those buildings." He jerked his thumb towards a number of office buildings further down the street.

Geddes panned the camera in that general direction. Smoke was billowing up from behind the buildings, and the crackle of gunfire could be heard. Red and blue flashes illuminated the grey clouds of rising fog as the strobe lights of emergency vehicles bounced off it.

Hannigan resumed his commentary as Geddes continued to film the general mayhem, "There seems to be near-constant gunfire now. We have heard automatic weapons being used, by which side is not currently clear, but there must have been deaths. Possibly many deaths." As he spoke, the street on the edge of his vision suddenly came alive as what seemed to be hundreds of people charged into view, screaming and shouting. In the first glimpse that Hannigan had of that terrible, writhing snake of bodies, he formed an instant impression of people running for their lives.

"And here... here it comes. Here comes the crowd. I..." Suddenly, Hannigan realised that they were in imminent danger of being mown down. He and Geddes flung themselves backwards, out of the way, flattening themselves up against a wall. A petrol bomb was thrown and exploded in the middle of the charging crowd. There were fresh screams, and people were trampled as they tried to get away from the flames. Geddes saw one man, whose clothes were on fire, frantically beating away at the burning fabric. But the mob rampaged on, and the man was knocked down and literally run over by the stampede. Hannigan watched breathlessly as some masked protesters peeled off from the main column and rushed into doorways. He saw hands move into pockets, and pistols were drawn. More people fled past him and Geddes. They remained squashed into place, hardly daring to breathe, all thoughts of reportage forgotten; this was now about survival.

The rush now seemed to be easing and slowing. People were falling out of the main rushing column all the time, darting into alleyways and ducking behind buildings, trying in vain to shelter behind parked cars. The shadowy masked figures in the doorways – mostly men, but Hannigan could see at least one woman amongst them – remained stationary, pistols held at the ready. Hannigan hardly dared draw breath.

And now, here came the enforcers – a mixture of police and army vehicles moving down the avenue behind the protesters and, behind them, police officers in full riot gear crouching behind the vehicles and scurrying along in their wake. More petrol bombs sailed through the air; some of them broke in front of the vehicles, but several smashed onto their windscreens, causing brief but intense plumes of dirty orange smoke. As the vehicles drew alongside them, the protesters in the doorways moved as one, and seemed to swing out into the street, loosing off a simultaneous volley of shots as they did so. Several of the riot police officers fell to the floor, some of them writhing and screaming; others were immobile. A number of other officers dropped out of the column and went to their fallen colleagues' aid. As Hannigan watched, the shooters seemed to fade away, to melt back and disappear into the crowd. Those guys were professionals, he thought, but professional what? Soldiers, police, some kind of secret service? Agents provocateurs?

This thought had only just started to cross his mind when there was a sudden burst of flashes from above and to his left and right. Then his ears rang with the insane chatter of automatic weapons firing. More police officers fell to the ground. He realised that the weapons were being fired from the buildings on either side of him, and then the full realisation dawned – this was a trap, expertly set for the authorities, and they had walked right into it.

Dana's Room

Dana let herself back into her room, walked in and flopped down on the bed. She lay there for a moment, knowing that her current position would be causing her exquisite red dress to rumple badly, but she didn't care. She thought back just a few hours, to when she'd last been in this room. Then, she had been excited for the evening ahead; she had looked forward to the thrill of the chase, the flirtations to come, the possibility of an illicit liaison. Now she seemed to be caught up in some kind of mini civil war. *Jee-zus*, she thought, not for the first time that evening.

She sat up and checked her mobile. Still no service. It now seemed almost certain that they were going to have to get through this without any kind of clue about what was going on out there. She threw the phone back down on the bed and wandered over to the window which overlooked the city. The streets and buildings beyond were still brightly light, but a pall of smoke hung over the downtown area of the city, and bright flashes kept throwing the scene into sharp relief. Even through the thick glazing of her window, she could hear crashing, shouting and gunfire.

As the shots rippled outside, she looked through the window at the panoramic view beyond. Even though the city lay spread out before her, she felt trapped. Trapped in this place. Slowly, she leaned her head against the window and closed her eyes as another time came back to her.

*

The trailer park in Lubbock. A warm spring day, a gentle breeze rustling the burr oaks and cedar elms that lined the edge of the park and detracted from the mess within it. Dana liked to lie on her back beside those great trees on days like this and squint upwards so that she could see branches and leaves, outlined against the brilliant blue of the sky, but so that the trailer park itself was out of view. She could pretend that she was somewhere else entirely. Sometimes she would see a jet making its way across that infinite blue expanse, trailing two or four pearly vapour trails, and she would wonder where it was heading, and what that place would be like. In her thoughts, wherever it was, it was always better than the trailer park. Anything had to be.

That day had started off like so many other Saturdays, her Mom waking at midday, with a raging hangover and it wasn't long before she started shouting and screaming at Dana. When her Mom was like this – which was most days – Dana couldn't do anything right, so she just tried to be quiet, to blend in, keep a low profile. As soon as she could that day, Dana snuck out of the trailer and made for the comfort of the trees, where she watched the scudding clouds and wished herself away from this place.

She lay there for a while, and then she heard the familiar rumble of Wade's pick-up entering the park. Propping herself up on one elbow, Dana watched the battered red Dodge driving past the serried ranks of dilapidated trailers with a sinking heart. An already shitty day was turning worse. The pick-up bounced along the grassy track until it reached the shabby trailer that she and her Mom shared. Wade pulled up, killed the engine and stepped out, taking a final drag of his Marlboro before crunching it out into the dirt beneath his leather cowboy boot. Under a dirty denim cap, his lank, greasy hair hung down to his shoulders. He rubbed a finger across his nicotine-stained moustache, spat out a ball of phlegm and then, hitching up his jeans, strode up to the trailer door, which he opened and entered without fanfare.

Wade hadn't seen Dana and she sank back down onto the grass with a leaden feeling in her stomach. The breeze rustled her hair. She lay there, making the most of what she knew would be her last few moments of peace today.

She heard the trailer door being flung open. "Dana!" Wade bellowed, "Get your goddamn ass in here now!" Dana sighed and reluctantly got to her feet.

"Now, Dana! Get in here, girl, or I'll whip your butt! I *will* whip your butt!"

Dana trudged across to the trailer, hating Wade that little bit more with every footstep. Life had been far from perfect before Wade showed up in their lives, but now it was getting to be unbearable. She couldn't wait to get out of here and escape to somewhere else. Anywhere.

She walked past Wade, and into the trailer, smelling the beer fumes on his rancid breath as she did so. Wade stepped back into the trailer after her, pulling the door of the trailer shut behind them both. Her Mom was still in her dressing gown, sitting on one of the threadbare sofas, leaning forward, looking pallid and tired and holding a cigarette in her shaking hand. Smoke from it curled up towards the trailer's yellowed ceiling.

"You got cleanin' to do, girl," Wade snapped. Dana sighed and started picking up some of the detritus that littered the trailer floor. Wade popped open a beer can and took a hearty swig, then opened another and passed it to Dana's mother, who gratefully accepted it.

By the time Dana had finished her chores, it was dark outside and her Mom was passed out. Wade carried her into her bedroom and then returned to the main room of the trailer, where Dana, her back aching, was tying up the last of the trash bags. Wade leaned on the counter of the kitchenette, beer in hand, watching her. She felt his eyes on her but tried to ignore him. She took out the trash. When she came back in, Wade took a long gulp of beer, then dropped the empty can onto the floor of the trailer.

'Missed one," he hissed, indicating the can.

Dana bent to pick it up and, as she did so, Wade grabbed her arm. He pulled her up, roughly and ran his stubby fingers through her dark hair. "You got one more thing to do for me, girl," he breathed. He kept a tight hold of Dana's arm with one tightly clenched hand. He reached his other hand down and started to unbuckle his belt.

Dana's heart was racing. She could feel the hot stench of his breath on her cheek. She stood very still.

"Get off me," she whispered.

"What's that?"

"I said get off me," she said slowly.

"Now who the hell do you think you're talkin' to?"

"Get your fucking filthy hands off me!" cried Dana, and she pushed backwards with all her strength. Wade, surprised, loosed his grip and staggered back a few paces.

There was silence for several seconds. Wade gripped his belt buckle. "Oh, you done it now, girl. You done it now," he said as he moved towards her.

*

There was a knock at the door. Startled, Dana lifted her head from the window, feeling where the glass had made a small indentation on her forehead. How long had she been standing there like that, replaying that day?

The knock came again, and she crossed the room. She was about to open the door when she thought about the circumstances under which she was currently in the hotel. She paused.

"Who is it?" she called.

"It's Ryan," came the answer. I'm with Nigel."

Dana opened the door and smiled weakly.

"Everything OK?" asked Ryan in a surprised tone. Dana didn't seem her usual bubbly self.

"I'm fine, hon," she grinned, although Ryan thought it seemed a little forced. "Just worried about all o'this, ya know?"

She gestured behind her to the window and the world beyond it.

"Yeah, I know, it's quite the adventure isn't it? Listen, Nigel and I just wondered if you'd like to come and join us? We don't like to think about you being on your own."

"Thanks," said Dana, "I'd like that." She collected her bag and followed her fellow flight attendants down the corridor.

Doorways

Shots continued to ring out, some bullets zinging off the army trucks and ricocheting crazily. *God knows where they are ending up*, thought Hannigan. The security forces were finding their feet again now, in some cases literally. The trucks had stopped their relentless push forward, and armed personnel crouched behind them, taking shelter as they knelt and took aim towards the top floor of the towering buildings around them.

Beyond the trucks, the crowd was much further down the avenue, out of the range of the shooting which was going on. The great mob had stopped its headlong rush westwards. Hannigan glanced over and could see that some of the protesters were taking the opportunity to leave, to get out of there. These were the people who had been caught up in a peaceful demonstration gone wrong, and they were desperate to be away. But he also saw the main body of the crowd pausing, as if for breath, gathering itself, spoiling for a fight.

Another volley of shots rang out and Hannigan pushed back automatically, seeking further security in the solidity of the shop door behind him. He looked across at Geddes, one doorway down from him. The sign above his friend's head announced that the doorway was to The Gumdrop Sports Bar, but it was dark within. A faded poster for the last-but-one Spider-man film was incongruously taped to the inside of one of the windows. Geddes was working on his camera, preparing to heft it to his shoulder; he had clearly had the same thoughts as Hannigan

He couldn't see any other TV crews in the street – they had to get this on camera. This could be a scoop.

"Dave, you filming?!"

"Rolling now, Steve!" Geddes shouted back. The noise was intense – the gunfire, the shouting from the security forces, sirens, helicopters, the low, bass braying of the crowd in the middle distance.

Hannigan looked left and right and then risked a quick dash over to Geddes' doorway. He started his shouted reportage.

"The protesters have been chased by the police and army through the city. We are now in the downtown area, where these trucks have been brought to a standstill in an apparent ambush. This…" he waved his arm in front of the camera, "… is now a shoot-out. There are what appear to be snipers in the buildings all around here, and they are trying to pick off the members of the security forces, who are now firing back. We have also seen people from within the crowd, usually masked, shooting at the police."

He paused for breath and let the wave of sound wash over the camera and microphone for a few seconds.

"It's no longer clear," he continued, "who is the aggressor here. At first, it seemed that a peaceful protest had been broken up by an extremely heavy-handed authoritarian state, but this ambush – this trap – that the security forces seem to have stumbled into must have been planned well in advance."

He wiped sweat from his forehead and made a cutting motion to his throat towards Geddes, who paused the camera.

"So, what now?" Geddes shouted.

Hannigan shrugged. "Wait it out, I guess."

Colin and Sarah

"So, what brought you to this side of the world?" Sarah Booth asked Colin.

"Work. A long time ago."

"What sort of work?"

"Finance. Futures, derivatives, stocks…"

Sarah laughed, "That sounds boring."

'Well, more boring than flying a plane, perhaps. But lucrative."

Sarah smiled again, "I'm sure it is."

They were sitting on the floor of the lobby, backs to the wall, alongside each other. Tony Johnson stood by the main doors, looking out at the street beyond, Lee Chung by his side. In front of them, Rob Mitchell paced, agitatedly.

"Sorry," said Colin, "I hope that didn't sound smug. It's just a fact of life – it's a high-pressure world, but the rewards can be amazing. I guess it's what's kept me out here all these years."

"That's OK. I knew what you meant." A pause, then "So… as a local, then, what's your view on what's happening? What do you think will happen next?"

Colin, who was sitting with his knees drawn up to his chest, exhaled a large breath of air through pursed lips. He considered for a moment before he spoke, "I guess this has all been brewing for some time. I didn't think it would come to this, though. There's just a fundamental dissatisfaction from a large part of the population of the city about the way that things are run. Democratic rights, freedom of speech…"

"Do they have a point?"

"To a certain extent. But then again, they get a really high standard of living. Look at some of the other countries in this part of the world that have those other rights in full – they're not doing too well for themselves. Standards of living are much lower than they are here. I guarantee you that most of those protesters wouldn't trade what they have here to move there in exchange for a few extra rights."

"So, you're not sympathetic, then?"

"I'm not *un-sympathetic*, it's just… they seem to want it all."

"Cakeism." said Sarah.

"Sorry?"

Sarah smiled. "Cakeism. Wanting to have your cake and eat it, too. It's one of those new buzz phrases in the UK."

"Ah, that would explain it. I'm not exactly down with the kids these days."

"So, where does it go from here?"

Colin rubbed his chin. "Hard to say, really. This government absolutely does not take any shit. From anybody. I imagine they'll throw everything at getting control back as soon as they can. Possibly brutally. Probably, in fact. But I don't think it'll last very long. They won't let it."

"That's not going to go down very well with the international community."

"Ah, this lot won't give a shit about that. They just do what they want, and to hell with the consequences. No, I think the next day or two are going to be messy and violent. That guy over there was right," he nodded towards Tony Johnson, still standing, as if on guard, by the doors, "We're better off staying put here and waiting it out."

Greta

"I'm hungry," Gaby announced.

She was sitting up on her bed in the Braziers' small suite, Tricia perched on the end of the bed, Greta seated on the chair in the corner. Graham, standing in the doorway, leaning against the jamb, looked at his watch.

"9 o'clock. Jesus, no wonder – we didn't eat anything." He suddenly felt hungry himself. Their pre-dinner drinks had turned out to be just, well – drinks. There had been no dinner, for any of them. Graham stalked through the rooms to see what he could find. A minute later, he had a small collection of biscuits and some chocolate bars and tubes of crisps, from the mini bar. He distributed them out between the others in the room, reserving the largest amount for Gaby and taking none himself.

"Graham, you must eat something too," protested Tricia.

"No, you take it," said Graham, "I'm not actually hungry," he lied.

"But Graham…"

"No, please - and you too, Greta," he said as his sister-in-law prepared to object, too.

Graham found bottles of water from the mini bar and from the kettle area and handed those out, too. Gaby hungrily tucked into her chocolates and biscuits. Somewhat sated, she wiped her mouth with the back of her hand. "When will this be over?" she asked.

"Darling, we just don't know," said Tricia, "I'm sure we're safe here, we just have to wait and see what happens."

"Yeah, right."

"What's that supposed to mean?" asked Tricia.

"Like, you saying we're safe here. We'll probably all be dead by tomorrow."

"Gaby, come on, don't be like that. We're all affected by this. It's a difficult situation but one I'm sure we'll come through. We've just got to stick together and be there for each other," said Graham.

"Whatever, Graham," said Gaby in a patronising tone, folding her arms as she did so and deliberately looking away from her stepfather.

Graham raised his eyes to the ceiling and walked out into the suite's main room.

"Gaby!" Tricia whispered urgently, "Don't be like that to Graham! He's just given you his food. Can't you just be civil to him? Just this once? Under these circumstances?" She had been facing towards her daughter and suddenly remembered about Greta, sitting in the corner. She spun around, "Oh Greta, I'm so sorry, you must think we're dreadful, arguing like this."

Greta, looking somewhat embarrassed, held up both her hands and gave a nervous little laugh. "Hey, it's families, Tricia. It's fine."

"Oh, Greta, thank you. It is wonderful to finally meet you, but who would have thought it would have been under these circumstances? It's so bizarre!"

"Well, that's true enough!" said Greta in a louder voice than was strictly necessary. She was glad to be able to help move the subject on and defuse some of the tension in the room.

"So, tell us about you and Colin," said Tricia, "how you met, what your life here is like. We'd love to know - wouldn't we Gaby?"

Gaby shrugged her shoulders and took a sip from her bottle of water. She had no interest in Graham's family. No interest at all.

"I'd like to know," said Tricia, "Tell me about yourself, Greta. Please."

So Greta did. She told Tricia about growing up in Switzerland, about university in Colorado and about her early work as a lawyer in Frankfurt.

"My goodness, you've travelled, Greta!" said Tricia. "I've never lived outside Lincolnshire. Well, apart from university. But even then, it was only Manchester, so not too far."

"Travel is great," said Greta, "but sometimes you just want to put down some roots. Look at me; I'm 42 and I've only just got married for the first time."

"So, yes, how did you and Colin meet?"

Greta thought back to the evening eighteen months ago when she had attended the gala dinner that the bank she worked for had hosted. It had been one of those hot and humid nights that she so associated with this city. The dinner had been a necessary chore, one of the relentless rounds of social engagements that she, as a senior lawyer for the bank, was expected to attend. So, she dutifully did, never eating nor drinking too much, meeting the right people, making the right number of connections, always projecting the safe, sensible, reliable face of the bank. Normally, she couldn't wait to gracefully excuse herself, head home to her tiny apartment, kick off her high heels and climb into bed. But, on this occasion, she had broken her own routine – after the meal and the toasts were complete, a breakaway group had suggested heading back to the penthouse that belonged to one of its number and, to her surprise, she had found herself agreeing to go along. She still didn't know why she had agreed to that, but she was glad that she had done - she was almost sure of that. *Almost.*

The breakaway party was an eclectic mix of men, women, business partners, romantic partners, different ethnicities, different sexualities, different generations. They numbered about twenty in total and she didn't know how everyone knew each other. To this day, she still didn't know what the common denominator had been, but the chemistry seemed to work, and the conversation and laughter flowed. Not to mention the wine.

When she thought back now, her abiding memory was of the rooftop swimming pool. It shone as the centre point of the whole space, its turquoise waters shimmering and lit ethereally from within, a ghostly blue light rising like a halo above it. Around the pool, the partygoers sat in easy chairs, sipped drinks and talked business in easy conversation, whilst music that Greta now knew Colin would describe as "chilled out beats" filled the background space.

The hot and humid night had continued, and it hadn't taken long for the first of the financiers to jump into the pool, clad only in his boxer shorts. Others had followed, and so had Greta, in fairly short order. Again, she had surprised herself this evening, this time by slipping out of her dress and jumping in, only able to do so because of the modesty of her underwear – after all, although it was fairly wild by her standards, it hadn't been *that* kind of party. She had felt liberated that evening, pulling great armfuls of underwater breaststroke whilst other guests acted more frivolously on the surface. She had also been grateful for having controlled her appetite at dinner.

Finally surfacing, she was smartly handed a glass of champagne by a neatly dressed man with close cropped, black hair and long sideburns. His hair was streaked here and there with grey. He smiled at her and she automatically took the drink and sipped it. It felt good after the unexpected exercise, and she felt giddy. Giddy with the scene, with the drink, with the promise of the future. At that moment, she felt that anything was possible - she was a successful, affluent, single career woman, and *anything* was possible.

Standing in the shallow end of the pool with one arm draped over the poolside, she drank from her flute and then chinked her glass against that of the man who had given her the drink.

She was a successful, affluent, single career woman... she was a single career woman... she was single. She was forty. Her head spun a little. She saw stars, but she wasn't sure whether they were in the sky or in her head.

Distantly, she heard the man say that he was called Colin. She heard a voice say that she was Greta. Somehow, she floated out of the pool, and they were talking. Somebody produced a towel, so that she didn't have to talk to him in bra and pants. He was chivalrous and courteous. She went home – alone – but with his number.

They met at a bar two days later and enjoyed each other's company.

A couple of days after that, they went to a restaurant and she still enjoyed his company, but a little less.

The following week, they went to one of the beaches, and she found his conversation a little dull.

Not long after that, he asked her to marry him. She said yes.

Greta said to Tricia, "Oh - we met at a party."

Decisions

"Is there anything to eat?" Rob Mitchell asked Lee Chung. The smart little hotel manager was standing at the empty reception desk, deep in thought, his chin cupped between the finger and thumb of his right hand. He looked up at the sound of Mitchell's voice and seemed, for a moment, to be a little startled.

"Ah, of course, I've been distracted by events. Let me speak to the kitchen staff – we'll prepare something to make sure nobody goes hungry. There will be no charge." He moved off towards the kitchens and Mitchell stepped across to join Tony Johnson by the doors. Johnson had his arms folded, feet planted firmly apart, and he was gazing into the middle distance with a worried look on his face. Beyond the doors, the night was bathed in a strange glow, punctuated by regular flashes. Outside, the streetlights were still on, illuminating empty pavements and roads.

"Heard anything?" asked Mitchell.

Johnson looked round at Mitchell and shook his head, "No, still got no comms. Everything's down – even the landlines."

"What about that?" Mitchell pointed to a walkie-talkie clipped to Johnson's belt.

"Nah, I can reach my other members of staff with this, but they're either all inside the hotel, in which case they don't know anything either, or they're at home and out of range. Or out there." He looked grim as he nodded towards the streets beyond the plate glass.

"Right." Mitchell looked out through the great pane of glass too.

"It's getting closer, though," Johnson said.

Mitchell looked across at the security man, questioningly.

"The demonstration. The riot. The battle. Whatever it is – it's getting closer to us."

"Are you sure?" asked Mitchell.

"Yeah – I've been here for most of the last hour. I can hear the sounds more clearly, and the flashes of gunfire aren't so distant. There's been a lot of gunfire."

"Shit."

"Yep."

"So, what do you suggest we do? Just wait it out, or is there something proactive we can be doing?"

Mitchell felt twitchy. His pilot's training told him to work problems, try alternatives, logically press on through the issues to reach a solution. Just standing around and waiting for fate to intervene didn't come easily to him.

"I'm not sure what we can do," said Johnson.

"Well, what about these?" Mitchell gestured in the general direction of the doors.

"What about them?"

"Plate glass, exposed. What happens if the battle ends up right out there? These things are gonna shatter if they take a bullet."

Johnson rapped on the glass. "I'm not so sure, they're pretty thick. But… you may have a point."

He looked out through the window again. "It's closer. Definitely."

He seemed to reach a decision. "OK, let's do it. Let's stay on the safe side. We'll barricade these doors. It might be an over-reaction, but…"

"… Better safe than sorry." Mitchell finished his sentence for him.

"Exactly."

Johnson looked around the lobby, casting his eyes over the various pieces of furniture. He made a mental inventory of the contents of the different rooms on the ground floor of the hotel. Finally, he turned to the remaining people in the lobby and held up his hands. In his deep, Essex-accented voice, he called for their attention and then he outlined his plans for barricading the doors.

On the Balcony

Graham was on the balcony. Possibly not the most sensible thing to do with what seemed like an incipient civil war breaking out all around him, but he wanted to clear his head. That girl was so bloody awkward. He felt, as he often did, at his wits' end with her. He took a drag on his cigarette – failed once more to stop, he thought – and looked out over the skyline. Down and to his left, he could see a pulsing glow. The din and clatter of the large-scale disruption was now very evident, too. It sounded very close now.

He thought about Gaby again. God, he'd tried; he really had, but he just didn't see what else he could do. The fundamental fact was that he wasn't her father, and she never let him forget that fact. *Would never let him*, he thought glumly. Guiltily, he inhaled deeply from his cigarette. Mind you, he thought, if you can't relapse into smoking with all this going on around you, when can you?

He thought about Colin, idly wondering what he was doing down in the lobby, who he was with. How bizarre, he thought, for the sister-in-law that, three hours ago he had never met, to now be sheltering with them in their room whilst his brother was locked into a hotel lobby three floors below. He shook his head at the way that events had transpired. Maybe they should have gone all-inclusive to Greece, after all. But still, this was turning into one hell of an adventure and when it was all over, he'd have a great story to tell to his bearded colleagues in Shoreditch.

War

Shots continued to be fired from the office windows. Hannigan could count at least five bodies lying motionless in the street, but he knew there would be more. Probably many more, and on both sides. The army trucks were still parked where they had stopped, but now he saw a new sight; rumbling down the avenue towards them were several armoured personnel carriers. They came to a stop just behind the trucks, and scores of soldiers jumped out, about ten from each one. The soldiers were kitted out in battle armour and helmets. The unarmoured police and soldiers who had been engaged in the firefight shrank back as their better-protected colleagues emerged. The armoured soldiers split into two groups, one dashing across to Hannigan's side of the street, and the other running to the other side of the avenue. The soldiers within the two groups fanned out and started entering the buildings facing onto the street. In some cases, they used miniature battering rams to force their way through doors; in other cases, they machine gunned shop windows, so that they shattered completely, and then they ducked through them, boots crunching on the shards of broken glass which popped and cracked beneath their feet.

Hannigan looked across at Dave Geddes, but they were on the same wavelength – the experienced cameraman was already filming. Hannigan shrank back into his doorway; no need for words on this one – the pictures would tell the story. As the last of the soldiers entered the buildings, Hannigan noticed that the turrets of the armoured personnel carriers were moving, rotating into position, so that they faced upwards, towards the windows where most of the shooting was coming from. In what seemed like a great roar of anger, the machine guns mounted on the turrets started firing, almost simultaneously.

God, thought Hannigan, *there was no going back from this, on either side – this was war.*

Ryan's Room

Dana sipped a cup of tea in Ryan's room whilst she nibbled at a biscuit and listened to Nigel waxing lyrical about his niece. She wasn't really hungry, but she felt that she needed to eat something; she could feel her blood sugar levels starting to ebb. She couldn't believe how things had changed in such a short space of time. Was it really only five or six hours ago that she had been sipping a cocktail by the pool and feeling horny? She glanced at her watch - 9.30pm. She certainly hadn't expected to be drinking tea at this time of the evening.

"… and the Head of Year has said that she's doing so well that Oxbridge may well – sorry, Dana, that's Oxford or Cambridge…"

Dana nodded politely.

"… that it may well be a possibility, and that she should definitely consider sitting the entrance exam."

There was a moment's silence. Dana waited for Ryan to chip in with something, but he didn't. "Awesome," said Dana, unable to think of a better response on the spur of the moment.

"So," she said briskly, "what's your favourite stopover?" She was desperate to steer the conversation away from Nigel's niece and onto something that she had even a vague interest in. She was beginning to wish that she'd stayed in her room.

"Ooooh that's a tricky one!" said Nigel.

"Definitely not this place anymore," said Ryan, and they all laughed.

"I can start if you like," said Dana, "It's not very original but I love Sydney. Sitting by the harbour with a chilled glass of wine, looking out at the Bridge and the Opera House. I think it's unbeatable, as views go."

"Well, I love San Fran," said Ryan, "for similar reasons – the Golden Gate Bridge. So iconic. Mind you, that is a city which does have a few other… attractions." He blushed at his own innuendo and Dana smiled indulgently. "And Nigel?"

"Hmmm… I'd sayyyy… Tokyo. Probably. No, definitely. Tokyo. I love the whole thing of being in a different culture, the hustle and bustle – all the rest of it. It's so – vibrant."

Dana nodded, "Yeah, Tokyo's cool. Been there a coupla times. Like it. Good choice."

She carefully studied her fingernails. Jeez, she thought, this is gonna be an even longer night than I expected. She dug out a small nail file from her bag and busied herself with a small manicuring session; that would while away some time. At least they weren't talking about Nigel's niece any longer.

Mezzanine

Plates of sandwiches had now arrived in the lobby, brought by kitchen staff who had remained at their workstations. As they were brought in, Sarah reflected on the altruism of the kitchen workers; whilst everyone else was standing or sitting around, nervously waiting for something to happen, these people had continued to do their work, to ensure that the people in the lobby didn't go hungry. She was impressed. What she hadn't seen was Mr Chung peeling off notes from a large wad and handing them out in the kitchen in a (successful) attempt to persuade them to make some refreshments for the guests.

Sarah wandered over to the plates and picked up a couple of the neatly cut triangular sandwiches. She didn't normally eat carbs in the evening, but needs must. As she took a bite, she wondered what kind of media coverage the unrest would be receiving back home. She thought about her parents, sitting in front of the TV in their cosy lounge in Telford. She wondered whether they would be watching and worrying. Maybe there was no coverage, though. If the government had pulled down all the comms, how would any news get out? But then again, she reasoned, if a huge city like this suddenly disappeared off the grid, wouldn't that be news in itself? Off the grid… she suddenly thought about the airport. My god, she wondered, are flights still coming in?

She couldn't see through the great entrance doors anymore; furniture had been piled up in front of them so that they were well and truly sealed in. A few of the guests milling around in the lobby had protested about that, but most had endorsed the decision. There was a certain feeling of security at seeing that great mass of material, piled up like a medieval bulwark. She was sure that if things took a serious turn for the worse, that barricade would certainly hold off whoever was trying to get in for a good long time.

But now her interest had been piqued by the thought of the aircraft due to fly into the airport. She looked around and spotted one of the twin marble staircases leading up, out of the lobby, past some large canvases and onto a mezzanine floor. Sarah quickly finished off the rest of her sandwiches, carefully placed her empty plate onto the table and trotted up the stairs.

The mezzanine floor that she found herself on gave onto a long corridor which was lined with what seemed to be conference rooms. She moved along, looking at the name plaques on the doors. They all appeared to be named after statesmen from the Second World War – The Eisenhower Suite, The Churchill Room, The Roosevelt Room. The corridor was enclosed on all sides by the conference facilities; there were no windows at all.

She stood for a moment outside the Eisenhower Suite and listened at the door. Silence from within. Carefully, she turned the handle and opened the door a crack. Inside, it was empty and dark. Excellent. Giving her eyes a few moments to adjust to the dark, she stepped in and carefully sidestepped around the big, central, oak table. Beyond the table was a large panoramic window, and she made her way across to it. Skyscrapers loomed above the window; it wasn't as good a view as she got from her hotel bedroom, but that was on the other side of the hotel, and this would be more than adequate for her purposes. She stood at the window and paused for a moment to get her bearings. *OK, the sun set over there, so that's west, which makes that way east. That's north, and the usual approach path given the prevailing winds here is from the south, so…* She quickly sketched a mental aviation chart and then looked over to the south to await the first aircraft. She checked her watch.

Standing at the window, waiting for the night flights to appear, she remembered her own first night-time approach. It had been at the air training school in Oxford and she had been flying a Diamond DA40 trainer. Seated alongside her instructor, she remembered tightly gripping the control column with a slightly sweaty palm. Everything seemed so different at night! She was already a competent solo pilot by daylight, but the night flying was a whole new ball game. She had turned for finals, catching a view of the M40 motorway below them, the white and red lights of the cars on it seemingly forming a long chain stretching off into the distance. The instrument panel was a glow of yellow and orange lights and, beyond that, as she banked, she could see the lights of the runway coming into view. "Very good," her instructor murmured, encouragingly. She eased out of the bank and finessed the rudder. She saw the runway sliding from its skewed position to level up, dead ahead of them. "Excellent, Sarah," from the man to her right. It was going really well, she knew it. Only a couple of minutes more and… And then something happened. She froze. She felt a strange sense of disorientation, of detachment. All of a sudden, she wasn't sure what she was doing, and she snatched at the control column, unable to remember what to do with it.

"I have control!" barked the instructor. Sarah sat there, almost in a trance. "I have control!" he repeated tersely.

"You... have control," Sarah said in a very quiet voice.

The instructor landed the aircraft without incident and they taxied over to the hangars. Sarah was shaking as she climbed out, and felt tears welling up in her eyes. She was sure that that was that. She'd blown it, pilot career over before it had begun. Countless hours spent working crappy jobs in supermarkets, pubs, even an ice cream factory and carefully harvesting the meagre income from them, just to be able to fund another hour of tuition – wasted. She felt sick. She felt embarrassed and ashamed. She'd found her level, and it was way, way below where she thought it would be. How would she face her friends? Her parents? How could she explain this? This... abject failure?

But the instructor smiled and patted her arm, his airborne clipped efficiency now gone. He walked her across to the office buildings and up to the canteen, where he more or less forced her to eat a Mars Bar and drink a cup of sugary tea. That was when she had burst into tears, burying her face in her hands, whilst the other diners tried to look away. The instructor – Bill – had spoken to her soothingly, had let her collect herself and had given her lots of words of gentle encouragement. She had never forgotten his kindness. An hour later, they were in the air once more and the scene played out again.

She levelled the wings, the runway slid into view, dead ahead of them, her hands dry and steady on the control column and throttle, and she had gone ahead and executed a perfect landing. The feeling of relief was almost overwhelming. She had never experienced anything like it, before or since.

Shaking off the memory, she brought her attention back to the night sky over the city as she gazed through the window, searching for navigation lights in the sky. A minute passed, then two minutes, then three. After she had been standing at the window for a full ten minutes with not a single flight leaving or arriving at one of the world's busiest airports, she was satisfied that the airport was not operating.

She slowly descended the stairs. The total absence of aircraft from the skies above the city had brought home to her the magnitude of the situation that they were now all facing. As she moved down the staircase, she thought about the chaos that would be unfolding for airlines and passengers. Aircraft in flight diverted to cities in other countries; those which had yet to take off, unable to; aircraft stranded at the wrong airports; long queues of irate, impatient passengers; flight schedulers tearing their hair out. The impact of the closure of this main international hub would be profound and it would radiate across the world, knock-on effect following knock-on effect.

Sarah reached the bottom of the stairs and walked over to Rob Mitchell, who was standing gloomily aloof from the other people dotted across the floor. Rob had his phone in his hand and appeared to be mindlessly playing some game or other. He looked up as she approached him.

"The airport's closed."

"What?"

"The airport. It must be closed. There are no flights coming or going. I've just been to check. I waited ten minutes, maybe more. Nothing in the air – except helicopters."

Rob whistled through his teeth, "Jeez, that's big, that's really big. It does make sense when you think about it, the phones, internet, TV all down. Why would they allow people to keep coming and going? Christ Almighty, where's this all leading to?"

Sarah knew it was a rhetorical question, but she couldn't help shaking her head, "Your guess is as good as mine. Who knows?"

<u>Chaos</u>

The crackle of machine gun fire from the turrets of the armoured personnel carriers stopped with a suddenness that took Hannigan by surprise. He felt his breath catch slightly and although there was still plenty of noise coming from all around them, the ceasing of the clattering fire seemed to have wrought a form of silence. He looked across at Geddes, who shrugged. He still had the camera running, and shifted his grip on it, wriggling his shoulder into a slightly more comfortable position.

Muffled shots and gunfire could be heard coming from within the buildings that surrounded them. Straining to hear, Hannigan thought that he could also hear faint shouts and screams. Then, without warning, a huge explosion rocked the top floor of the building directly opposite. Brick, mortar and glass erupted out of the side of the office block in a dirty grey convulsion of debris and cascaded down into the street below like an obscene waterfall. Rubble and bricks started to hit the street; some hit the trucks and APCs. The night air became hazy with dust.

"Jesus fucking Christ!" yelled Hannigan. Geddes had flinched where he stood, but still kept the camera rolling.

Now, orange flames were licking at the gaping hole left by the explosion. A helmeted head briefly emerged through the hole, appeared to rapidly survey the street scene below, and then quickly withdrew.

For a moment nothing happened, save for the crazy column of dust particles which was now swirling around in random convection currents in front of them.

And then, it happened all over again. This time, from behind them. Detritus rained down, directly in front of the two journalists. They squeezed themselves back, against their doorways to avoid being hit. Hannigan's heart was racing, hammering away in his chest like it wanted to get out. He was wreathed in sweat, the hairs on his arms standing upright, and his whole body seemed to fizz with a combination of excitement and terror. He tried to grab a big lungful of air to calm himself, but just sucked in dust for his troubles. He bent over double, coughing and spluttering.

The explosions had set off burglar, car and fire alarms, which shrilled pointlessly into the night and now there was further noise, as the APCs and trucks started up and began to move further down the avenue.

He became aware that Geddes was shouting something at him. "… here, Steve. Now!"

"What?" Hannigan shouted back.

"We need to get out of here – get down there, see what's going on."

"What the fuck just happened here?"

"Special forces. Those guys from the APCs." He tried to reiterate his point, bellowing into Hannigan's ear. "They must have been special forces. Found the shooters, blew the crap out of them."

Hannigan nodded.

"We've gotta move now, Steve, the action's moving on."

Hannigan looked down the main road in the direction that Geddes was pointing. The rear of the personnel carriers looked like a solid wall of armour to him as they moved away, down the street towards the bulk of the civilian protesters. "Okay."

"We need to get behind the crowd," Geddes was shouting again, "Get around the APCs somehow."

Hannigan nodded again. Geddes had a good nose for this kind of thing. He was happy to follow his cameraman's advice.

"Come on," Geddes picked up the camera from the floor where he'd laid it, took a quick look from the doorway in both directions, and then set off to his left. Hannigan glanced right and then followed him. There was no more shooting in this part of the street, but they still crouched low as they scurried, keeping close into the buildings, until they came to a four-way intersection. Geddes darted off the main road, taking the left hand crossroad, and Hannigan followed.

Immediately, things felt more subdued. There was still a lot of noise from the main avenue, but it was deadened to some extent by the buildings between them and where the battle was unfolding, now seemingly entering a second phase. Hannigan felt a slight lessening of tension; this felt safer, and they started to jog along in a more upright fashion. He was glad to be able to straighten up somewhat; his lower back was aching from the crouching. They scuttled along, past dark shops and offices. Some of the shopfronts had been smashed in; it looked like there had been some looting. Not a surprise, thought Hannigan, there were always chancers and people on the make in any situation like this. Why should this be any different, just because this whole situation had started off as legitimate protests? Well, seemingly legitimate – now he wasn't so sure after having watched the security forces stumble into what he was sure was a deliberate trap. They trotted past a Tesla showroom, its windows intact, three cars cocooned inside, still shiny and new, looking totally incongruous amidst the chaos that was unfolding beyond the showroom's windows.

He saw Geddes' plan now; dive down this road, then pick a side street running parallel to the main avenue, head down there for a reasonable distance, then make a right and emerge back out onto the avenue into the main crowd, ready for the confrontation with the army. It was dangerous but, by god, it would make for good TV.

And then a shot rang out. Geddes, running along in front of Hannigan, went down. He pitched forwards, the camera flying out of his hand and arcing forwards and to the side, landing roughly in the middle of the road. Geddes sprawled onto the ground, facedown, arms outstretched in front of him. Blood oozed onto the pavement.

"Dave, shit, Dave…" Hannigan came to a stop, panting heavily. Another shot rang out and Hannigan pushed himself back against the shop window behind him.

"Oh, fuck! Oh, fuck!" With a rising sense of panic, Hannigan looked around them. There was a small alleyway a few metres in front of them. On the floor, Geddes lay still, but moaning quietly. Hannigan took a quick, forlorn, glance at the camera lying completely exposed in the road. For a moment he hesitated, then, crouching, scuttled around the cameraman's immobile body, grabbed him under the armpits and started to haul him to the alleyway. There was the zing of another shot. Instinctively, Hannigan ducked, but he had no idea where the shot had come from, or how close it had been to them. He continued shuffling backwards, dragging his friend along. An ugly, sticky smear of blood stained the pavement. Another shot. This time there was a second, smaller crack of sound, as some masonry was stripped away from a building by the bullet. It sounded close. Hannigan was sweating profusely, with both fear and effort. He managed to manhandle Geddes around the corner and into the alleyway, where he carefully lowered his colleague's chest back to the floor. He gently placed the cameraman's head on the ground, carefully turned to one side. Geddes was still moaning in pain.

Hannigan put his hands on his knees and tried to suck in air. His heart was still racing, like a jackhammer in his ribcage. He had no idea whether they were safe, but this would have to do, for now at least. He wondered what he'd do next, but his mind was a blank. To his surprise and disgust, all he could think about was the camera, abandoned in the street, all of the unbelievable footage that they'd captured contained within it. As he stood, gasping for breath, beside his injured colleague, snipers in the area, he was out of ideas.

Mitchell's Thoughts

He folded his arms as Sarah walked back across the lobby, towards that Colin guy. They seem to be getting on well, Mitchell thought, and he frowned. He wasn't envious; he didn't want to be friends with Little Miss Perfect, but he didn't like the thought of somebody else striking up a friendship with her. He watched as Sarah sat down next to Colin and said something to him. The conversation was all one way and looked earnest and intense. She would be telling him about the airport closure, he thought. He didn't like Colin. Not since that moment in the bar when he'd challenged his authority.

And you are? he'd asked him in front of the rest of the bar when Rob had suggested staying together in the lobby. Who the hell did this guy think he was? Some jumped up financier going up against an airline captain, a man who was used to having the safety of 500 passengers in his hands. Mitchell felt the rage taking hold inside him, a steady, resentful loathing of the man sitting on the floor on the other side of the lobby, talking to his First Officer.

To calm down, he walked away from where he was standing, crossed the lobby and entered the bar that they had vacated several hours previously. This was where Dana had also ridiculed him, he thought bitterly. He had thought he might have been screwing that bitch by now; instead, she was back in her room and he was alone in an empty bar. He felt anger welling up again and went and sat down at the sofa they had been using earlier. Their glasses were still all there, some still half-full. He stared morosely at them, one with lipstick stains around the rim, and then he thought about the jacket hanging in his wardrobe, the jacket with the envelope in its breast pocket.

It was the first time he'd thought about the envelope for several hours. That was one good thing about civil war, he thought, it took your mind off the fact that your wife was divorcing you.

It hadn't particularly been a surprise to get the letter from Harriet's solicitors; they'd been separated for a couple of months, but it was unpleasant, nonetheless. She was divorcing him on the grounds of his adultery but, to be honest, it could have been unreasonable behaviour, irreconcilable differences or any number of other reasons. Take your pick. But yes, he had shagged around a lot – so what? It was often there for him on a plate when he was flying, and he took full advantage. Harriet didn't know the half of it, but he had thought that he'd get away with it. He thought that she'd probably had her suspicions, but she was never able to prove anything. That was one benefit about being abroad a lot – it was easy to cover your tracks and get away with whatever you wanted to. And then he'd gone and stupidly left his phone lying around and, although she couldn't access it, Harriet had been walking past it laid on the kitchen worktop when it pinged with a WhatsApp notification, and she'd looked down and… well, it had all unravelled after that. And she'd gone mental, absolutely fucking mental.

He knew she'd take him for as much as she could. He shivered. Christ, it was going to cost him a fucking fortune. He thought about their lovely house, on the edge of the Surrey Hills. That was bound to have to go – she wouldn't settle for a pay-off, she'd want as much as she could get, and she would want to see him suffer, as well. And she certainly wouldn't accept the holiday cottage in Carcassonne in lieu of the Surrey house. Then he thought about the girls. Surely she wouldn't try to stop him seeing Tabitha and Megan. Or would she? Harriet could be a real vindictive cow when she put her mind to it. He might have been a lousy husband, but he was a good Dad. Other than hardly ever being there, of course. But he always bought them presents, didn't he, from wherever he was in the world? That must count for something, surely?

He thought about the house again, his pride and joy. Please, please, don't let him lose that. In his life-long battle against Simon, that wonderful house was the one thing that he could point to as evidence that he'd come out on top. Just his luck to have a fucking cardiac surgeon for an older brother. Being an airline captain would make you the big star and the biggest earner in most families, but not in his. But Simon just had a flat, a central London flat admittedly, worth an absolute fortune, but he didn't have the beautiful home that Rob did. God, if he lost it, that would be an absolute disaster. He wondered if it was too late. Maybe, when he got home, he could try and make it up to Harriet. He could probably turn this situation of civil unrest to his advantage, use it to get her sympathy. He could play it all up to her, how he had had time to think things over, regret his behaviour, and would she give him another chance? It would all be bollocks, of course, but, if it helped save the house, it was probably worth trying. If he could just persuade her to call off the dogs, he could move back in, they could play at happy families for a while, and he might, just might, be able to salvage things.

He started to feel better about the situation. He stood up from the sofa and took a little walk around the bar. He could feel his mood lifting perceptibly. He wondered what Dana was doing now. He wondered if she was still in her room, and what she was doing. He thought about her naked body, about the curves and valleys that he'd possessed for a single night last year, and he felt a surge of lust.

Tony

Tony Johnson surveyed the barricade that they'd put up against the doors. It wasn't bad, he thought, considering it had been constructed by a rather motley crew of hotel guests and staff, with even the teenage girl lending a hand where she could. He had overseen it all, and he was reasonably pleased with the results. Sure, it wouldn't repel an invading army, but it would certainly act as a deterrent to anyone trying to smash their way in. He hoped it wouldn't come to that, but there was no way of knowing how far this unrest would spread, how the next few hours would unfold. It could all end with the authorities regaining control, or the opposite could happen, and things could totally spiral out of control. Maybe they already had done. *That was the thing, no comms and absolutely no idea what's going on in the outside world.* He checked his phone again. Still no signal, still no wifi. He took that to mean that events were continuing to unfold out there. Surely, once they had stabilised the situation, the government would want to be broadcasting its message out to the people, to try to crush any further dissent.

Through a gap in the furniture barricade, he glimpsed some new flashes of light coming from high buildings in the streets beyond the neighbouring skyscrapers. He recognised them immediately for what they were. The flashes sparked his memory and he was suddenly a young man of twenty again, cold, wet and nervous but with adrenaline coursing through his veins as the battle began.

The first thing he saw was the four Harriers, coming in low and fast from the east as the first etchings of dawn started to appear in the leaden sky behind them. They screamed over A Company's position and then arced away, back into the disappearing night, chased by ferocious anti-aircraft fire. He didn't see the bombs drop, but he certainly saw them hit – great swathes of gloopy mud and turf flung up into the air, accompanied by vivid orange and yellow flashes and then, seconds later, the sound rolling in across the bleak terrain to where they were dug in on Darwin Hill. It was an awesome display of firepower, and, as he lay there in the muddy cold he felt a swill of both pride and encouragement as the jets headed back towards the aircraft carriers.

Soon it would be their turn. He shivered, and not just from the cold, as he stared ahead of him down the hill, at the territory that they would have to cross shortly. And then it came, the order to advance. He and his fellow paras started to make their way stealthily down the hill, cradling their weapons carefully. But they had clearly been spotted; a massive volume of machine gun fire from about 400 metres away opened up on them as they descended. They fired back sporadically, and he loosed off several volleys himself, but their firing seemed to simply draw attention to their position, and each time they fired, they received a greater volume of Argentine fire in return. The CO motioned to them to cut the fire, and they continued to move forwards. To his left, a man was hit, and he rolled in agony as a fellow soldier went to his aid. But the advance continued, and soon they were in the line of gorse bushes at the bottom of the hill, and they had a little more protection than they had had earlier. That was where they stayed for the next hour or so, as operations unfolded around them. Other companies were attacking the Argentine positions from different directions, and the SAS were in the mix too, moving around in the shadows and stirring up their trademark blend of agitation and chaos. But A Company were held up; a sniper with a good position, and clearly a great line of sight, firing into their midst. He lay there on the mossy turf, damp percolating up from the ground, through his fatigues and into his skin, to leave him absolutely frigid with cold. His fingers were numb and he could barely feel the Self Loading Rifle, even though he was gripping it tightly. Pinned down by the sniper fire, he risked looking left and then right. All he could see were his colleagues' heads, kept well down. To think that one man with a single rifle and a good aim could hold up an entire company of the British army like this, it was incredible. And then the news came over the field radio, that the Colonel had bought it. "Sunray is down," was the terse message that they heard, and none of them could believe it. He had gone down charging a machine gun post, trying to unblock the logjam, so that the assault could get moving again. And all the time, Johnson and his company were frozen in place by a single frigging sniper…

And now he watched through the gaps in the furniture as the snipers fired from the tower blocks and he wondered which side they were on and thought about the poor bastards below them who were copping it.

On the Stairs

Ryan and Nigel were now discussing their favourite crappy reality TV shows, and Dana could stand it no more. "Well, gentlemen, it's been a pleasure, but I guess I'm feelin' kinda cooped up now and Dana needs to stretch her legs." Her colleagues stopped their discussion, and Dana couldn't help feeling that they looked a little hurt. "Need to see if I can grab a bite to eat, too," she added soothingly, "That biscuit ain't gonna keep this gal going for long!"

She slipped out of the room, leaving the two flight attendants to their discussion and walked down the corridor. She paused beside the lift and wondered whether it was worth taking a chance. Surely she wouldn't be unlucky enough for the electricity to go off whilst she was descending three floors in an elevator? But she might be. For a moment, she hesitated and then walked towards the stairs.

As she started down the steps, she wondered what it would be like to be trapped in the elevator if the power was lost. Mind you, the thought of the electricity being cut was only in her mind because of Rob suggesting earlier that it might happen. The thought hadn't occurred to her – maybe that was why the captains were paid the big bucks, to think ahead and see problems like that before they arose. Rob. An image of his surly but handsome face flashed into her mind as she descended. God, what had she seen in him that time last year? She couldn't say exactly what it was that she looked for in the men and occasional women with whom she chose to share her bed, but she knew it when she saw it, and it certainly wasn't anything that was on offer from Rob. She chose to think of that episode as an aberration, a momentary loss of control, something to chalk up to experience. It wouldn't be happening again.

She reached the bottom of the staircase and, trying to banish thoughts of *that* night from her mind, exited into the lobby.

Gaby

Gaby was hungrily tucking into another sandwich when she noticed the female flight attendant reaching the bottom of the marble staircase. There were two stewardesses staying in the hotel that Gaby had noticed. One was in the corner, talking to the female pilot and the barman. She smiled a lot, and Gaby had heard people calling her Rachel, but this was the glamorous one, the one with the long, dark hair and Mediterranean complexion. Gaby watched as she sashayed her way across the lobby, flashing Gaby a smile as she went. She was wearing a long red dress and looked immaculate in it, despite the fact that it was now bearing a few creases. Looking around the lobby, Gaby had noticed that most people were starting to look crumpled and dishevelled, as they sat or stood around wherever they could, but not this woman. She looked like she was at the Oscars, not trapped in a building with fighting going on all around.

The thought of the fighting sent Gaby's stomach lurching, and she put down the rest of her sandwich. She suddenly didn't feel hungry anymore; she felt frightened again. She approached Tricia, "Mum, can we go back? Back to the room?"

"But, darling, we've only just got back down here."

"I'm scared, Mum,"

"Yes, but we all agreed, sweetheart, that we'd be better off down here now. Get something to eat, stay with the others, maybe find out what's going on out there."

"Yeah, but…" Gaby gestured towards the makeshift barricade which was now blocking the doors, "… I mean, just look. It's scary."

"I know, I know, but I think at this point, we are better off with everyone else. It's…" Tricia consulted her watch. "… it's 11.15 now and we need to be prepared and ready for whatever may happen in the next few hours. And we'll be better off down here, I'm sure. I felt cut off and out of the loop in the room."

"But we're down here now and we still don't have any idea what's going on!" protested Gaby.

Graham walked over. "I think your mum's right, Gaby. It was the right thing to go back to the room for a while, but now I think we're better off down here. I honestly do."

"Get lost Graham," Gaby snapped.

Graham knew what was coming next.

"You're not even my Dad!"

He felt his fists clench involuntarily and he ground his teeth together. He took a moment and then continued, in what seemed like an artificially calm voice.

"I *know* that Gaby. But the final decision is that we stay down here. At least for now."

"Fine!" shouted Gaby. Her fear had left her now and had been replaced instead by a seething anger and resentment. She stalked into a corner of the lobby and stood there, hands on her hips, staring moodily into the middle distance.

Graham blew out a large breath of air in exasperation. Tricia laid a consoling hand on his arm.

Little Milestones

Back to the hotel. It was the only viable option. Hannigan looked up and down the alleyway, Geddes on the ground at his feet, slowly writhing with the pain. There were definitely no safe options here, he thought, and watching the battle with the snipers had shown him that there could be hostiles anywhere and, anyway, who could they trust? Who had even shot Geddes? He no longer had any idea which side was in the right and he felt that he had lost track of events. Things, to use the vernacular, had spiralled out of control. So, it had to be the hotel.

That was the one place where they could have some trust and, because they had been doubling back on themselves ever since they had first encountered the frontline of the battle, it must now only be a few hundred metres away. He looked down at Dave Geddes, clutching his abdomen and moaning softly. Suddenly, a few hundred metres felt like it was going to be a hell of a long way.

Still, nothing for it. Shots and shouts were still ringing out in the main avenue a couple of blocks behind him, but, for now it seemed quiet in this alleyway. He considered for a minute and thought that it was probably safer to head down it than to risk going back out onto the side street where the sniper had shot Geddes. Satisfied that he had at least the prospect of a plan, he turned to his prone colleague.

"Dave, Dave, listen. We gotta get to the hotel, man. We can't stay here. I'm gonna lift you up, and we're gonna have to walk it. We should be safe the way we'll go, but I ain't lyin' to you pal, it's gonna be tough to get there, so I need you with me, my man. I need you with me."

Geddes was still moaning softly in the grip of his agony, but Hannigan saw him make the briefest of nods.

He looked down at the ugly red stain which had spread across Geddes' lower abdomen. "OK, good man. But, first – we gotta do something about that – you're bleeding." They had left the hotel in a rush, just running straight out into the night in the clothes that they were wearing. That meant that Hannigan was wearing very little that could easily be converted into a bandage or tourniquet. He looked around. The alleyway was empty and dirty; he couldn't see anything usable. Well, nothing else for it, he thought. He pulled off his shirt. It was heavy with sweat; he caught a strong whiff of his own body odour as he removed it and involuntarily wrinkled his nose. Not great, he thought. Not very medically hygienic, but it's either this or... He forced himself to stop his train of thought. He had no wish to imagine Geddes bleeding to death in front of him. Instead, he busied himself with his first aid responsibilities. He rolled up the shirt so that it formed a kind of cigar shape, and he gently pushed it into Geddes' stomach area and then used the shirt's sleeves to tie it around the cameraman's back. Geddes called out as Hanigan tightened the sleeves.

"Sorry, sorry, man. I'm so sorry, but we've gotta stop that bleeding. OK, we're gonna make a move. Ready? All set?"

He stooped his bulk and hooked his arm around Geddes' neck, then he raised himself, slowly bringing the pair of them to their feet.

Geddes let out a gasp of pain as they did so.

"I know, I know, Dave. We gotta do this, though."

Finally upright, Hannigan swayed for a moment under the unfamiliar weight, as Geddes sagged by his side. "OK, let's go." They started to lurch down the alleyway. Geddes tried to help, tried to get his feet moving but it was a real struggle for him, and of no real help to Hannigan who was puffing and blowing before they had moved even a few metres.

They passed some overturned rubbish bins and random pieces of stray litter as they moved down the alleyway. It stank of piss; a plastic bag sauntered past them on the gentle breeze, a thin cat pausing in its endeavours to watch them suspiciously as they passed. Tall buildings crowded them on either side, and Hannigan was alive to the possibility of further snipers. The buildings were largely dark; Hannigan didn't know whether that was because they were empty, because any inhabitants inside were keeping their heads down – literally – or whether it was cover for shooters. No matter – they had no choice, and the pair staggered on.

After a few minutes, Hannigan decided they needed to rest. They stopped in a place where one of the buildings had a large expanse of concrete wall rather than any windows or doors. He carefully lowered Geddes down, into a sitting position and paused a moment to catch his own breath. He looked down at the cameraman; he looked in a really bad way, pale, clammy and the tourniquet was leaking. After a moment or two, he felt able to continue, and he manhandled Geddes to his feet again, keenly aware that each time he made his colleague go through that manoeuvre, it was putting more strain on his abdomen. They set off again.

Little milestones, thought Hannigan, little milestones. He saw a telegraph pole approaching. *OK, when we get there we'll be doin' really well.* They reached it, although it seemed to take an eternity, and moved past it. *OK, next one?* Hannigan looked up. They were approaching an intersection, where a small side road crossed the alleyway. *OK, when we get there, that's good progress.* They staggered on. Away to his right and behind the buildings, the clamour of the fighting seemed to have intensified. The glow of fire could be seen in the night sky, even beyond the tall buildings which hemmed them in. Then, as they approached the intersection, two figures suddenly appeared out of the shadows. They wore dark clothes – black trousers and bomber jackets. They both wore scarves across their lower faces, and both were carrying baseball bats.

Lose-Lose

Lee Chung retired to his office and closed the door behind him. He often retreated here when he found the stress of running the hotel getting to him, and it almost always had the desired effect. This was his sanctuary, and although it was functional rather than luxurious, modest rather than spacious, it was the space where he always felt that he could get away from things. The walls, whilst not officially soundproof, certainly provided good insulation from the comings and goings in the lobby beyond and afforded him time to think and get things in perspective. Even on a normal day or night, he would retreat here several times during his long working hours to mull over a problem or try to see an issue from a different angle.

But tonight he felt differently. There was no problem to solve, and there were no matters to be resolved. This was the most difficult night of his career and he was a mere observer, a passenger. He and Tony had done everything they could to manage the situation; they had briefed the guests, they had tried to manage overcrowding in the lobby, he had arranged free food for everyone, they had barricaded themselves in. All he could do now was wait. Wait and see how events unfolded.

He felt like he was in a lose-lose situation. If events took a turn for the worse and the hotel was damaged, or guests injured (or worse), he would be devastated. He loved this hotel; it had been his life, his pride and passion since joining its staff over thirty years ago as an assistant receptionist. He had worked his way up to his current position, and he had remained popular whilst doing so. He hadn't had to tread on any toes or make any enemies on the way up; that wasn't his style. He'd done it all on his own terms, fairly, treating his employees courteously and with respect, and often with a smile on his face. But, on the other hand, if events outside calmed down, if the government regained control or made its peace with the protesters and the sun rose in the morning on a city where law and order had been restored, he would have been shown to have over-reacted. The Board of Trustees would want to know why he had sanctioned the use of the hotel's ground floor furniture to be wrecked as it was piled up as a barricade, why guests had been prevented from entering or leaving, and why they had effectively put the hotel onto a war footing. In those circumstances, he was sure he'd have to resign.

He thought about the other hotels in the city and wondered what they were doing. Was it business as usual there, or were they too in lockdown, waiting and wondering what the rest of the night had in store?

He sighed, retrieved the chunky remote control from the leather-bound top of his desk, aimed it towards the TV and jabbed at a few buttons. "No signal" was the response which came back at him from the screen, whichever channel he tried to watch. Still no news, then. He opened the top drawer of the desk, took out the little tin that resided in there and popped a breath mint into his mouth and then, still feeling as though he had the weight of the word on his shoulders, he stepped back out into the lobby.

Time Drags

He looked at his watch; approaching midnight. Time was dragging for Colin. His back ached and his thighs were stiff after hours of sitting propped up against the wall of the lobby. He had tried moving back to the bar, with its plush sofas, but he had felt completely isolated in there. No, uncomfortable though it may be, he felt he was far better off in the lobby, with the hotel management, the other guests and, once more, his wife.

He had felt a slight trace of annoyance when Greta had decided to go up to the other Braziers' room with them; he had thought that she would have chosen to stay with him but, then again, he did appreciate her showing solidarity with his brother's family and, let's face it, it relieved him of his responsibilities in that direction. Still, she'd reappeared with the rest of Graham's family a few hours later, apparently when the sulky kid had got too hungry, and now she was back in the lobby, sitting alongside him as the hours dragged by.

"Tired?" he asked her.

Greta gave him a weak smile. "A little. Bored, mainly."

"Yeah, me too. Just got to wait it out though, I suppose."

He checked his watch again; it had barely moved. This time of night, he'd usually not long have been home from the office. Just time for a quick whisky nightcap and a final check on the global financial markets which were still open before heading to bed for, if he was lucky, five hours sleep before getting up and repeating the whole damn thing over again. What a life, he thought. He didn't often take the time or have the time to stand back and think about the lifestyle he led. Now that he did, he started to see what a treadmill he was on, and he began to wonder whether it was all worth it.

He looked up at the vaulted roof above them. He thought about his apartment, with its ocean views and state of the art gadgets within it, about the well-equipped gym within the block it was situated in, about the swimming pool on the roof. But he also thought about its tiny size and its extortionate cost. He thought about the amount of time he spent there compared to the amount he spent in the office. And he thought about the fact that he and Greta barely saw each other and, when they did, seemed to have little to say. His mind moved onto imagining the apartment block and what was happening to it right now. In one of the most central districts of the city, it would have been right in the path of the protesters as they poured out of the park, chased by the army. God knew if it was still there, and if it was, what kind of shape it was in. He tried to imagine the protests ending, order being restored and everything going back to the way it was. He tried to imagine him and Greta, at home in the apartment, spending more time together. He found he was unable to do it.

He stopped staring at the ceiling and brought his gaze back to the lobby. Across the way, Sarah Booth was talking to Rob, the captain. Her boss, he supposed. He'd only met the woman a few hours ago, but he felt like they'd been getting on famously. Unbidden, the thoughts came to him – imagining sharing the apartment with Sarah. He saw her in the kitchen, on the balcony, in the pool with him, in his bed. His and Greta's bed.

Greta looked across at him. "Penny for them?"

"What?"

"Your thoughts."

"Oh… nothing. Just… mulling things over."

He felt himself reddening. He thought that his innermost thoughts must be written all over his face.

Encounter

Hannigan stopped in his tracks, also jerking Geddes to a stop as he did so. Geddes let a quiet moan. Shit, thought Hannigan, this is it. We're screwed.

He had already sweated more this night than he had even thought possible but, still, he felt a trickle of cold fear run down his back.

The two masked men had also stopped at the sight of the two Americans. Disconcertingly, Hannigan suddenly had a fleeting image in his mind of how they must look to the men with the baseball bats - the big, black uninjured one; the thin, white wounded one. He wondered what they must be thinking, and exactly what role they had been playing this evening. He wondered if they spoke English.

"Hi. Press." He shouted. "TV. News."

The two men stared back, their eyes emotionless above their masks.

"Do you speak English? We're from the TV News. PNN. My colleague – he's badly injured."

The masked men continued to stare. There was no lighting in the alleyway, but the moon was nearly full and cast the scene in a silvery glow. One of the men moved out of the glow and into shadow; the other remained in place. His right arm – the one holding the baseball bat – twitched.

"Please. My friend. He's been shot. Please, we need to get through. We're not armed." He held up the arm which wasn't supporting Geddes and put his hand into an open palm gesture. It was only half a hands-up signal but he hoped it was universally understood.

The man in the middle of the alleyway continued to stand his ground. Say something, you asshole, thought Hannigan, *anything*, but all he said was "Please."

The two masked men exchanged glances, then the one in front of them moved forward till he was just in front of Hannigan, who was still standing, supporting Geddes' weight. "TV?" the man asked.

"Yes, we're from PNN – Planetary News Network. The American news channel."

"American?"

"Yes." Hannigan knew that was a statement which could go either way. People caught up in these situations either thought Americans were heroes or devils; there was never any middle ground.

The man in the shadows advanced forward, to stand alongside his colleague. "America. Good," he said. Hannigan could have cried with relief. He now needed to get past these clowns, to get Geddes to the hotel. He gestured down the alleyway. "I need to move him. I need to get him to safety." Geddes felt like a dead weight on his arm now. Hannigan just wanted the masked men to move out of the way so that he could continue his lurching journey, but then the man in front of him spoke again. "We help," he said.

Kiev

Dana walked out into the lobby and looked around. She spotted Rachel Bray and Sarah Booth; they were talking to the barman from earlier on and she decided to head across and join them. She walked past the family of three who had also been in the bar earlier and felt that the teenage girl was staring at her a little too intensely. Dana smiled to herself; she was well used to attracting attention when she made an entrance. She gave the girl a beaming smile as she passed and hoped it provided her with a little encouragement; the poor kid was no doubt terrified at the way things were unfolding.

She was good at reassurance, she thought to herself. She'd dealt with her fair share of nervous flyers, drunks and otherwise distressed passengers during her career. Colleagues often said that she had a great way of dealing with the general public, one that always put people at their ease. And then there was the glamour, of course; women wanted to look like her, men, and not a few women, just wanted her. She'd certainly come a long way since those trailer days in Lubbock, since her Mom and that creep Wade. She thought briefly about them and wondered if they were still together or, indeed, still alive. And then she banished them from her thoughts because tonight was tough enough without thinking about those losers.

She reached Rachel, Sarah and the barman that she'd been flirting with earlier. Oleksanders, he was called, she remembered. He was thin and tall to the point of being gangly. He had close cropped, brown, hair and stooped slightly when he spoke, no doubt mainly due to his height. Her colleagues smiled and said hi. Oleksanders gave her what seemed to be a courteous little bow, and a gentle, slightly enigmatic, smile, "Hello Dana."

"Hey, you remembered my name; that's impressive – we were only talking for a coupla minutes."

"I wouldn't forget."

His words hung in the air; she wondered whether he was implying he had a good memory or whether he wouldn't be able to forget her. She loved the ambiguity.

"Well, that's very sweet of ya… Oleksanders."

A slight upturn of his lips at that and another slight nod of the head. Wow, this guy communicated a lot in gestures.

Sarah turned to her, "Oleksanders was just telling us about a time in Kiev that was similar to this."

"Oh yeah, what happened?" asked Dana.

"I wouldn't say it was exactly similar," said the barman. "I think, unfortunately, this is more serious."

"No shit."

That enigmatic smile again.

"It was the protests in 2014. The government was overthrown. Yanukovych's government. The Revolution of Dignity, we called it. The government wanted closer ties with Russia, the people wanted to be closer to Europe. There were protests. Lots of protests, but it was peaceful, as we have seen here. Until tonight. And then, like here, all of a sudden, fighting broke out. Nobody was sure who started it but there was a very big fight with the police. Very big. Very bad too. It lasted several days."

"Sounds bad."

"It was. Many people were killed. Many more injured."

"And what was the outcome?"

"Well, the people won. Sort of. Yanukovych was kicked out. Gone. He was very corrupt man, and best gone. We get new government, honest government, but…"

He paused, and Sarah said, "… but that's when the fighting started in the rest of Ukraine?"

"Yes. That was worse. Lasted for years. Is still going on, in fact."

"Jesus, and you say this is worse?"

"In the city, yes. I think so."

"How so?"

"More people protesting, many thousands more, I think. And the government is much more…" He searched for the words.

"Oppressive?" offered Sarah.

"I don't know this word. Er… tough. Hard."

"Yep. Oppressive," said Dana.

"OK, oppressive. At least I learn a new English word tonight." His eyes twinkled and they laughed.

There was sudden shouting from across the lobby; they all looked round. It was the teenage girl; she was shouting at her parents. Then she stalked across to a corner of the lobby and stood there, defiantly.

"Whoops," said Rachel as they averted their eyes and returned to their conversation, "someone's got their work cut out over there."

"Must be tough for her, though," said Sarah. "God, I'm not sure how I'd have coped in a situation like this when I was fourteen or fifteen."

For a moment, Dana was back in the trailer park. In her mind, she vividly saw Wade's battered red pick-up. "You'd cope," said Dana in a small voice. "You'd have to."

*

The Greyhound bus station was noisy and dirty, its fetid air a rank mixture of diesel fumes and stale sweat, but Dana couldn't be happier to be there. She thought about Wade and wondered if he was still sitting on the floor of the trailer, nursing his balls. She smiled grimly to herself as she remembered his howl of pain after her well-aimed kick, and her smile deepened as she thought about putting the rock through the windshield of the Dodge Ram on her way out. Yep, Wade was a dick and he'd got exactly what he deserved. She swore she'd never see him again.

She wondered whether her Mom had come round yet, and what Wade would tell her when she did, how he'd explain Dana's absence, or if he'd even try to. Or if her Mom would even notice – or care. *She must care*, she told herself. Deep down, beneath the booze and the pills, surely her Mom loved her? But she never showed it if she did. Ever.

Dana checked the departures board and clutched her ticket a little tighter. The bus to Austin left in ten minutes; good, she would be on that bus and she didn't intend to see Lubbock again – not for a very, very long time. She didn't know what she would do when she got to Austin; all she knew was that, whatever it was, it had to be better than the trailer park. She knew something else, too; whatever life had in store for her, she was going to make a success of it.

*

"I suppose," said Rachel. "Dana? Hey, Dana? Earth calling Dana?"

"Oh, sorry, Rach. I was miles away there."

Literally miles away, she thought. Climbing aboard a Greyhound bus and gettin' the hell ou of Lubbock.

The Restaurant

The view through the cracks in the furniture left a lot to be desired, and Tony Johnson wa anxious when he didn't have as full a picture as possible about what was going on. That wa true at any time, let alone tonight as the city outside was gripped by anarchy, so he decide to head upstairs. He knew exactly where to go; the open part of the hotel might only hav three stories, but the attached tower had plenty of vantage points, even if it was still construction site.

He trotted back up the stairs, first to the Mezzanine level, and then carried on, upwards. He was heading for the fifth floor where a large restaurant was starting to take shape. From what he remembered from tours of the construction work, it had large windows which gave expansive views. His view would still be blocked by some of the skyscrapers, but at least it would let him see over the roofs of some of the lower level buildings in the area. He made a brisk pace as he went; he might be 57 now, but he prided himself on his physical fitness. His 6'4" frame had barely an ounce of fat on it. What was that line that Michael Caine said in *Get Carter*? You're a big man, but you're out of shape... well, he was a big man who was very much in shape.

On the third floor, he walked down a long corridor, squeezing past a life-sized Greek statue which had tastefully been positioned in front of the entrance to the building work. He ducked under a plastic sheet and turned onto the tower's main staircase. Reaching the fifth floor, he entered the shell of the restaurant. Inside, it was dark, the only illumination coming from the lights out on the landing and the glow of the nearly full moon, hanging orb-like in the sky, a silent witness to the carnage taking place below. There was also a ghostly orange flicker dancing off the walls of the restaurant. He knew what this was without having to look; it was the flicker of the flames from fires which were burning across the city. He moved past the empty bar, his shoes clacking noisily across the concrete floor. He stood in front of the big windows and let his eyes adjust to the darkness. The city beyond started to come into focus. The scene was awash with light; streetlighting remained on and many of the tower blocks, save for a narrow strip down the length of the main avenue, were still lit. Huge neon billboards dotted around the city garishly advertised soft drinks, athletic footwear and the latest must-have electrical goods. But from across much of the metropolis, great clouds of smoke drove blankets of grey up into the clear night sky. Many fires burned in pockets. One neighbourhood seemed to be completely ablaze. There was some evidence of fire crews working in different areas, he could see, but most of the flashing blue and red lights, he knew, would be from police vehicles. He could see that any intervention by the fire services would be a token; the scale of this devastation was massive, and he shook his head sadly. He had come to love this city and considered it his adopted home. For all its faults, which were many, it had a charm and a vibrancy that he had enjoyed and embraced. Now he watched as it convulsed, and he wondered what the future had in store for it.

His eye was drawn, once more to that thin line of darkness, cutting down the central avenue. He corrected himself; it wasn't dark, it just wasn't lit. Within that narrow strip, on either side of the towers lining it, he could see great crowds of people running and surging. There were cars, trucks and armoured personnel carriers down there. Brief explosions flared as petrol bombs were thrown and he saw the intermittent flashes of gunfire. The view confirmed what he had suspected. He was now in no doubt that the battle was moving closer to the hotel. He estimated that the edge of the fighting was now only a few hundred metres away. Having seen enough, he turned away from the window, swiftly made his way out of the restaurant and headed back down to the lobby.

Below him, and unseen, four men were making painstakingly slow progress down an alleyway parallel to that main avenue.

<u>Hope</u>

"That one," Steve Hannigan gestured with his head towards the hotel. He started to feel the first waves of relief; maybe they were going to make it after all. Once more, he felt a massive debt of gratitude to the two strangers. They had one arm each around Geddes' shoulders, whilst Hannigan cupped his knees and lower back in an improvised chair. Clad now in the white T-shirt he had been wearing beneath his outer shirt, Hannigan could feel Geddes' blood trickling onto his bare arms. Christ, how much blood had the guy lost? It must be at least fifteen minutes now since he was shot, and the bleeding had barely seemed to stop ever since.

The two men helping to carry Geddes nodded in unison as Hannigan indicated the hotel. They were still wearing their masks but seemed to be easily coping with their burden. The four of them emerged out of the alleyway and onto the side street that led to the hotel. Hannigan felt a pang of worry; it was on a street just like this that Geddes had been shot. He wished they could hurry up, but he knew that the impractical shuffling they had started five minutes ago was as quick as they could all go.

Like some kind of giant crab, they scuttled along the street, towards the hotel. Hannigan's eyes kept flicking nervously from left to right and back again, as they went. The street was empty of pedestrians, and there didn't seem to be any movement off to the sides, either. That gave the newsman a measure of confidence, but the constant sound of the clashes unfolding behind them reminded Hannigan that this remained a very dangerous situation.

Finally, they reached the entrance to the hotel. The two masked men helped to carry Geddes up the steps; once at the top, Hannigan ducked away from supporting his friend's weight to run ahead and rap on the doors to request them to be opened; he was sure they would still be locked and that that security goon would still be there, refusing to let people come or go. But as he approached the doors, he saw that the situation had changed since he had last been there. Where, once, there had been huge panes of glass, giving a view into the luxury within, now those glass doors were blocked from the other side by chairs, sofas, tables and, seemingly, any other manner of furniture which had been to hand. Feeling sickened and worried, he ran up to the doors and tried to peer within. There were lights on inside the lobby and the light was penetrating through the cracks and chinks of the piled-up furniture, but he was able to make out very little from within. He beat against the glass with the palm of his hand and called for help.

Behind him, the two masked men continued to support Geddes between them, but they looked across at each other and, then, over at Hannigan with increasing consternation. The sounds of violence beyond seemed to be intensifying.

Hannigan beat at the door again. "Hey, anyone there? We need help, we're guests! We have a badly injured man out here. Please help us!" He peered through the small crack once more. He thought he could see the shapes of bodies in the area on the other side of the barricade, and he sensed some movement, but there was no direct response to his hammering on the door, or to his shouted pleas.

He beat at the door again, with increasing desperation. "Help! Help us out here! Let us in... please!" He heard a muffled noise behind him, and then a groan. He looked around. The masked men were in the process of carefully lowering Geddes to the ground. Geddes moaned again, his ghostly pale face beaded with sweat and creased with agony. Their burden safely deposited, the men turned and walked down the marble steps at the front of the hotel.

Hannigan was caught by surprise. "Hey, what the... hey – don't go!" The men were now walking at speed back down the side street they'd just come down. Then Hannigan found himself wondering what he would do if they did come back. Would they expect to come into the hotel with him and Geddes, if they could find their way inside? Would the hotel admit them? Who even were they? In the last quarter of an hour, neither man had showed any sign of dropping their scarf mask; neither had said a word since that phrase – "We help" – had sent a surge of relief through him. Maybe it was for the best if they disappeared back wherever they had come from, back to engage with the disruption in whatever manner they had been doing earlier. He still had no idea if they were peaceable demonstrators, agitators, or men on a mercy mission. He just knew that they had acted like angels for him and Geddes. He didn't need to know what their role in all of this was. As he watched them disappear into the shadows, he saw one of them retrieve the baseball bat from the inside of his jacket, where he had stowed it prior to helping his colleague. Not only did he not need to know what their role was, he thought, he didn't want to know. He knew he wouldn't see them again.

"Thank you. Thank you both so much!" he hollered after them.

He didn't know if they heard him, or if they would understand him if they did, but he hoped that the sentiment registered on some level with them; without them, he was sure, Geddes would have had no chance. He looked back at his friend. He looked dreadful, his pallid complexion looking more sickly and grey by the minute. Hannigan turned back to the doors with renewed determination, and beat on them with a vigour born of the greatest frustration he had ever known.

<u>In the Lobby</u>

"There's somebody out there! Somebody's trying to get in!" Gaby's frantic screams echoed around the lobby, and the hubbub of muted conversation ebbed as heads turned towards her. "They're out there!" she shrieked.

She had been standing by the barricade for a few minutes, having vacated the corner that she had occupied, arms folded, since her latest bust-up with Graham. The corner had perfectly suited her need to quietly seethe, but then, she found that her stepfather, talking to that airline pilot, had gravitated a little too close to her, and she wanted to be as far away from that creep as possible – so she had moved on. But now, her squabbles with Graham seemed secondary. Now, her anger had dissipated, and the fear that she had felt earlier had returned. She had heard beating on the door, muffled by both the thickness of the glass and the piled-up barricade, but she had definitely heard it; *they*, she was sure, were trying to break in… whoever *they* were.

People across the lobby were looking over at her. She saw the big security guy coming across purposefully. "What's happened?" he asked her sharply.

"Out there, I heard it – banging on the door. Someone's trying to get in, I'm sure! Oh my god, I'm so scared!"

"OK," said Johnson with a crisp ring of authority in his voice, "try to calm down please. You've done really well; thanks for letting us know. Maybe it's best if you move over there for a while." He indicated the far side of the lobby. Gaby was starting to shake now and she was glad to see Tricia coming across to her. Tricia grasped her daughter's hand and shoulder and guided her away from the barricade.

Johnson addressed the rest of the lobby. "Everyone – quiet please."

What conversation there had been trailed off as the assembled lobby obeyed the natural authority in his voice. Johnson leaned in towards the barricade whose construction he had supervised earlier. And there it was… an insistent beating on the glass door and – there – above the muffled thuds, the sound of a man's voice, insistent and hurried. Crouched with his ear against the furniture, he tried to make out any words, but he couldn't; all he could detect was the urgency in the tone that came from beyond the glass. He shifted position and placed one eye against one of the gaps in the barricade. He closed the other eye and squinted. It was hard to make anything out, but he thought he could see movement on the other side of the doors.

"OK, please, there is no need for any panic, but there does appear to be somebody outside…" There was a rumble of concern from the people scattered across the lobby, "… but we are going to use the security cameras to review the situation. Please remain where you are and, I repeat, there is no need for anyone to panic."

"You can't know that!" he heard somebody shout, but he already had his back to them as he moved across to the steps to the basement and descended them, two at a time.

He flung open the door to the security office and rushed across to the bank of black and white TV screens which occupied one wall. In front of the screens was a computer keyboard, and he urgently tapped away at it, alternately glancing from the keyboard to one of the screens, which was labelled "FRONT VIEW" in stark white block capital letters. The view on the screen began to change as he manoeuvred the camera into position.

As the camera swung around, he saw the image on the screen shift from a view straight ahead and move towards the view slightly to the left-hand side of the main entrance. As the camera panned, he caught a glimpse of a prostrate body; he was about to stop the camera's rotation and move it back to zoom in on the body lying there, when he caught sight of movement on the extreme left of the picture. Ignoring the person on the floor, he continued the camera pan, and it brought into view a large black man who was repeatedly raising his arm and beating his hand against the doors. Johnson brought the panning action to a halt and leaned in closer towards the screen. He narrowed his eyes a little as he squinted at the image; he recognised the guy, he was sure of it. Then it came to him – he was looking at the man who had been trying to get back into the hotel hours earlier; the TV journalist who had wanted to get back in so he and his partner could borrow a car.

He zoomed the camera in. The man's face – etched starkly in black and white – looked anguished. Johnson quickly panned back across to the prone body beside the journalist; the injured man looked absolutely stricken. He quickly computed what must have happened – the journalists out on the streets, trying to get the story; and, then, either a shot, a petrol bomb, a knife – somehow the guy on the floor had been attacked and incapacitated. He'd seen enough; he raced back upstairs, into the lobby and looked around him. He saw Captain Mitchell and the father of the teenage girl who'd alerted him to the men outside. He shouted across to them, "Captain, Sir… I need help please – could you come with me?"

Both men looked up, almost simultaneously. "Injured guest… outside," he called, by way of the briefest of explanations. The two guests hurried across towards him, "What's going on?" asked Mitchell.

"It's the two journalists who are staying here," said Johnson, "They're both outside. One looks like he's in a very bad way. We need to get them inside."

"But…" Graham Brazier looked towards the barricade.

"Follow me," said Johnson simply. He set off into the bar that they'd vacated hours earlier, Mitchell and Brazier following on his heels.

They moved through the empty bar, and Johnson led them behind the counter. Behind a small ante door was a little storeroom, filled with various stores and supplies. At the rear of this room was a door; Johnson stepped across, produced a large bunch of keys, and unlocked it. "This way," he said, tersely, ducking through the door. Brazier and Mitchell exchanged glances and then followed him through.

Outside, Graham Brazier found himself in a small alleyway. One side of it was lined with a number of silvery barrels – beer supplies for the bar, he thought. The night air was sticky and humid; the sounds of clashes in the downtown area were very evident. Johnson headed up the alleyway, skirting to the left of the beer barrels. "This leads to the front of the hotel," Johnson called. Graham followed the big security man, Mitchell, the airline pilot, following along beside him.

Johnson led them around the corner of the hotel and out onto the front. The exterior of the hotel seemed largely as normal to Graham - the flags of several nations hung limply from their flagpoles in the still air; the drop-off semi-circle of road right in front of the hotel was quiet and unoccupied. But, as Graham looked around, there, right in front of the main doors, was a man lying on the floor and, turning to face them, was the big journalist who had been in the bar earlier.

"Thank god, please help us – we need to get inside," he shouted. He was almost tearful. "My colleague – he's been shot. He's in a very bad way."

Johnson quickly assessed the situation. "OK, come on, let's get him." The three of them advanced and, between them, shouldered Geddes' weight. Hannigan came alongside and helped support the cameraman too. "Thank you," he gasped.

Between them, the four men carried Geddes down the alleyway and on through the door, into the small room adjoining the bar. Johnson kicked the door shut from the inside and, allowing Hannigan to take more of Geddes' weight, broke off from the stretcher party to step over to the door. As Brazier and Mitchell moved the injured man through to the bar, Johnson opened the door and moved back out into the alleyway. He grappled with one of the beer barrels and manhandled it inside, and then repeated the procedure with a second. Then he closed the door, locked and bolted it and shifted both of the barrels into place against it. Satisfied that the door was now secure, he went out through the bar and into the lobby beyond.

First Aid

Dana had been preparing to help treat a casualty from the moment that Rob, along with the two other men, had left the lobby. Rachel was by her side, for once grim faced rather than full of fun, and the two of them waited. Dana mentally ran through her flight attendant's first aid training and prepared for the worst; she didn't like to speculate on what might have happened out there.

Within minutes there was a clattering sound from within the bar, then Rob and the squat, balding man who was part of the family of three emerged, supporting the injured journalist between them. Dana's breath caught in her throat as she saw him; he looked absolutely dreadful – a band of glutinous crimson cut across his abdomen and his face was like a great, sallow moon. The two men laid the journalist down on the floor of the lobby and Dana and Rachel dashed across to see how they could help.

Some of the other guests moved over too, but they mainly seemed to be concerned rather than able to offer any practical medical help, so Dana went to work. She was senior to Rachel and knew that she'd had more training than her colleague, and that Rachel would defer to her. All other thoughts fled from Dana's mind and she focused on the injured man as she knelt beside him.

"Hi honey, my name's Dana. Can you hear me? What's your name? Can you tell me your name?"

There was no response. Across the room, the large black man who'd come in off the street with the injured journalist looked up from where he was being tended to by one of the hotel guests. "Dave Geddes," he panted. "His name's Dave Geddes."

Dana bent close to Geddes' nose and mouth. She felt the faintest of breaths on her cheek and then checked his wrist pulse. Faint, but it was there. Relieved, she turned her attention to his bloodied abdomen. The rags of a torn shirt clung pathetically to the man's midriff. Although far from perfect, it was still helping to staunch the blood to some extent, but she knew it would need to be replaced immediately.

"Rach," she said, "Can you get a new tourniquet?"

Rachel sprang up and looked towards Oleksanders, but the barman was ahead of her and was already rushing back into his bar. Seconds later, he emerged with a first aid kit, which he handed over. Rachel snapped it open and rooted through the contents, finding the largest bandage, some scissors and a small bottle of surgical spirit. She passed them across to Dana, who was gingerly starting to remove the stained shirt from around Geddes' midriff. Fresh blood oozed and mixed with the congealed crusts of dried blood outlining a gaping hole in Geddes' gut. There were some gasps, and some of the onlookers turned away. Dana glanced over at the cameraman's head; his eyes were closed, but she could see a very slight rise and fall in his chest. Pressing down hard with the bandage that Rachel had given her, she staunched as much of the blood flow as she could.

"OK, that's held it for now, but gonna need another one of these, and something much bigger – a towel or part of a sheet?"

Tony Johnson darted away. There was silence across the lobby, tension thickening the air. Very faintly, from outside, the sounds of battle and violence could be heard.

Johnson returned with several white towels and a large white bedsheet. Dana glanced up. "The sheet," she said simply, "A long strip, say six inches wide." Johnson nodded and set to work with a knife he had also produced. Dana looked up at Rachel. "OK Rach, need you help now."

Rachel nodded and knelt on the other side of Geddes, directly opposite her colleague. "Bandage," said Dana. Rachel handed her another large bandage, which Dana quickly swapped with the first one, holding out the bloody chunk of material for somebody to take. She felt it being taken out of her hand.

"OK, Rach, keep the pressure on; I'm gonna swab, then tape." Rachel pressed down and Dana removed her hand. Decanting some of the surgical spirit onto a cleansing pad, she carefully wiped around the edges of the wound, gently easing away some of the pressure tha

Rachel was applying in order to do so and then letting the weight of Rachel's hand fall back into place as she moved on. After she had circled the wound with the pad, she held that out, and felt that removed from her grasp, too. Taking the scissors, she snipped several lengths of tape and then used that to secure the bandage.

"Ease off, Rach." The British flight attendant slowly removed her hand from the bandage; no blood leaked.

"OK, good. Sheet."

Tony Johnson passed her the strip of sheet. "Need to ease him up," said Dana, "Careful, now."

Johnson and Rob Mitchell stepped forward and, between them, inched Geddes' midriff off the floor. The cameraman gave a slight moan. Dana was able to pass the strip of sheet under his body and bring it back around, so it acted like a cummerbund. She pinned it in place.

"OK, that should do for now. That should stop the bleeding, at least."

She gradually got back to her feet, her red dress now smeared in several places with a different shade of scarlet. "Well done, Dana," called Sarah Booth.

"Yes, well done," someone else called.

Somebody started to clap and within seconds, others started to join in. As Dana dusted herself down, the lobby, which seconds before had been museum quiet, rang with applause.

Hannigan's Story

Steve Hannigan took a grateful swig of water from the bottle in front of him. He was seated in front of Lee Chung's desk. Lee Chung himself stood off to one side, whilst Tony Johnson occupied the seat behind the desk. The Englishman spoke first, "OK Steve, just tell us what you saw going on out there. It could help us form a plan."

Hannigan nodded and brushed some dried spittle from his lips. He looked tired beyond words, his eyes red and bloodshot, his white T-shirt stained, torn and hanging loose.

"It's bad out there. Real bad."

Lee Chung steepled his fingers in front of his nose, nervously awaiting the reports of what was taking place in his beloved city.

Hannigan continued, "I ain't seen nothin' this bad before. Ever." The last word was like a brutal piece of punctuation.

"OK, so specifically..." coaxed Johnson.

Hannigan drank greedily from his bottle again.

"OK," he walked over to the map on the wall. "We are..." he searched for the hotel's location. Johnson and Chung walked across and joined him.

"The hotel's here," said Johnson, indicating their location on the map.

"Right. OK, so…" Hannigan examined the map, and found what he was looking for, "So, this avenue here…" he jabbed with his finger, "this is a fucking war zone."

"Meaning?" asked Johnson.

"Snipers, APCs, petrol bombs, machine gun fire, SWAT teams, some kind of plastic explosive being used. Lots of people killed, many more injured."

Johnson was momentarily speechless; Lee Chung's steepled fingers sank onto his nose, and he inclined his head a little. This was worse than he had feared – far worse.

Hannigan was continuing. He traced his finger down the route of the avenue. "It's moving down. Down here, getting closer. It would be about here…" again, he stabbed at the map, "where Dave was shot. We were trying to get around the back of the protest by going down one of these side streets. I didn't see exactly who shot him, but it must have been a sniper."

Johnson examined the map; the street in question was only a few hundred metres away.

"It's a battle," said Hannigan, "There's no other word for it. Never seen anything like it before, not in Iraq, Somalia, nowhere…"

"It's close," said Johnson.

"Yeah, and gettin' closer. The police and army – they're pushing the protesters back this way. They'll do that, and then they get to a point where the protesters dig in and there's another round of fighting. Then I guess they'll keep on pushing."

"But why?" asked Lee Chung, "Why keep on pushing them further into the downtown area?"

Now Tony Johnson was the one gesturing at the map, "That's why," he said, his finger tracing a circle around the general location of the hotel. "Look at the lack of side streets around here compared to further up the avenue, and then behind them, there's just the sea. My guess is that they're pushing them down here to corral them into this area between the buildings. They wouldn't be able to get away or make any more trouble by ducking down side streets and then popping back up again to attack from the side. They'll be trapped."

"And they'll be right outside the goddamn hotel," said Hannigan.

<u>Respect</u>

Dana was cleaning herself up in the ladies' toilets. Standing at the sink, she scrubbed the blood from her hands and cleaned her dress as best she could. She splashed water onto her face – To hell with the mascara now, she thought. As she looked into the mirror, she saw the door behind her open. Tricia Brazier walked in. She saw Dana and stopped.

"Oh, hello. I… saw what you did out there. You were amazing."

For once, Dana felt sheepish. "Oh, hey – er, thanks."

"I couldn't have done that. You were so… steady. So… confident."

"I didn't feel it," Dana lied. "We get pretty good first responder training, though. Guess it paid off." She picked up a napkin from the neat stack by the sink and dried her face with it.

"If that man lives, he'll have you to thank."

"Unfortunately, I think it's a pretty big 'if'. He's very sick; he needs medical attention as soon as possible but I don't see how he's gonna get any. Not any time soon, anyhow. But we've done what we can for him. It's out of our hands, now."

"I suppose. I'm Tricia, by the way."

"Hi. Dana. That your daughter that's with you?"

Tricia blushed a little. "Yes. Gaby. This is all very hard for her."

"I'm sure."

The two women stood in silence for a moment, then Dana slowly dried her hands. "Well, I better go see what my guys are up to. Check they're lookin' after Dave OK."

"Of course. Well, thank you again for everything that you did."

"You bet." Dana scrunched up the napkin and threw it into the waste bin. She ran her hand through her long, dark hair, smiled at Tricia and walked out.

Tricia watched Dana go. She continued staring in her direction long after the door had closed behind her.

<u>Confrontation</u>

As Dana walked back out into the lobby, she saw the door of the manager's office opening at the same time. The manager walked out, along with Tony Johnson the security guy and Hannigan the reporter. They all looked deeply worried. Dana walked across to where Dave Geddes was now lying, on a makeshift bed of sheets and blankets. Rachel was by his side. She looked up as Dana approached.

Dana jerked her thumb in their direction. "Those guys don't look happy."

"God, no, they don't. Rob's going over to see them – look."

Dana turned; Mitchell was walking across to the three men. "Well, what's going on?" she heard him ask abruptly.

Tony Johnson stopped as the pilot intercepted him. "Rob, let's not..."

"I asked what's going on?"

"Can we not do this here please?"

"Not do what here? You need to bring me up to speed with what's happening."

"I'm sorry Rob, but I don't *need* to do anything. The safety of the guests and staff is the prime concern, and that's what we've just been discussin."

"Are you aware that I am well versed in dealing with high pressure situations?"

"Yes, I am."

"And?"

"And my answer remains the same – that the security of the hotel and the people within it is key."

"I demand that you tell me what's going on."

"Right, Rob – please can you step into the office for a moment?"

Johnson pivoted on his heel and walked back into Lee Chung's office. Rob Mitchell followed him, glowering, as heads within the bar turned to watch them go past.

"Close the door please, Rob," Tony Johnson's tone was menacingly polite. He stalked behind the desk and stood there, leaning over it slightly, fists planted into the leather top as Rob Mitchell closed the door behind him.

The pilot started first, "Right, you need to tell me…"

Johnson cut him off. "What the hell was all that about?"

"What?"

"Out there. What the hell were you playing at?"

"I need to know…"

Johnson interrupted him again. "Let me ask you this. Let's say you're flying your Jumbo…"

"Airbus," Mitchell corrected.

"… your Airbus, and you lose an engine. What do you do?"

"What?"

"What do you do?"

"We work the problem, follow the checklists, fall back on the simulator time. Deal with the issue. Why?"

"You have a snappy little phrase, don't you?"

"What are you talking about?"

"Yeah, I first heard it in the Falklands. The pilots of the Hercs used to say it when they were talking about trouble. You know the one I mean?"

"What? Aviate, navigate, communicate?"

"Yeah, that's it exactly. So, you get a big problem. First thing – you aviate; keep the aircraft under control, yeah? Second…" Johnson was ticking these off on his raised fingers, "… you navigate; once you've established control, work out where you are and where you're heading. Third, communicate. Only with the first two accomplished do you communicate to air traffic control or other aircraft."

"What is this shit, Tony? What are you talking about?"

"Guess where we're up to in this checklist, Rob? We've aviated… we're in control of the hotel – just. We're safe, for now. We're in the process of navigating – we're trying to find out where we're heading. We are not yet communicating, because we haven't sorted out the first two."

"But I…"

"So, let me take you back to this scenario in your – *Airbus* – Rob. You're an engine down, and you're still trying to navigate. I'm guessing that, at that point, the last thing you need is a passenger demanding information about what's going on, right in front of the other fucking passengers." By this point, Johnson was jabbing his finger down onto the top of the desk; his lean face was reddening. "Am I right?"

"How dare you speak to me like that? I'm a guest in this hotel..."

"Feel free to file a complaint against me. If you're alive to do that, then I will have done my job."

Mitchell was also now red in the face.

Johnson continued, "What we absolutely cannot afford to do is panic the people out there." He pointed beyond the closed door. "This situation is deteriorating. Fast. We tell people what they need to know, when they need to know it and if we need your help, we'll ask for it."

Mitchell went to say something but Johnson cut him off. "But I'm a reasonable guy, and seeing as you ask..." Johnson pushed himself up from the desk, moved out from behind it and walked over to the map on the wall. Without waiting to see if Mitchell had joined him, he waved his hand around the general area that the hotel occupied on the map, "... we think the battle has moved down here. The army is kettling the protesters into this space, which just happens to be around the hotel. There's a whole world of crap going on out there, and there's sod all we can do about it. So we either choose to scare the guests half to death, or we leave them in blissful ignorance and just tell them what they need to know. Satisfied?"

"Not particularly," Mitchell had now recovered his composure. "There's one thing you haven't mentioned yet - what's the plan?"

Johnson glared at Mitchell. A small globule of spittle had coalesced at the corner of his mouth. "The plan?"

"Yes, come on man, the plan. What are we going to do?"

Johnson looked at Mitchell with incredulity. "I would have thought that was pretty obvious. We stay put. We hunker down, wait it out."

Mitchell barked a short, mirthless laugh. "What? That's it? Sit and wait? Just sit around on our arses until the civil war arrives right outside the hotel? It would be funny if it wasn't so serious."

"Do you have any better ideas?" snapped Johnson.

This time, Rob Mitchell didn't answer; he was thinking.

Fear

Colin walked over to his brother and rested his hand lightly on his shoulder.

"How are you doing?"

"Yeah, OK," said Graham, "getting tired now I guess."

"Me too. I was wondering about trying to get some sleep but I don't think I'd be able to, and judging by the look on those guys' faces," he nodded towards Hannigan and Lee Chung, "there's nothing good about to happen."

Graham looked across in their direction but, at that moment, was distracted by a loud bang. He quickly looked over to his left, and saw Tony Johnson marching out of the manager's office, his face ruddy and angry. The door was still rattling in its frame.

"Jeez, what's gone on in there?" wondered Graham.

"Dunno. He was in there with the airline captain, Rob."

"Doesn't look good, whatever it was."

Graham turned his attention back to Tony Johnson. The Head of Security was walking across to Hannigan and Chung again. He reached the other two, said something to them and then the three of them moved into the corner where they continued their discussion.

As Graham and Colin watched, Lee Chung stepped away from Hannigan and Johnson and raising his voice, called for the attention of the people within the lobby.

"Ladies and gentlemen, could I – ah – have your attention for a moment please?" There was a brief buzz from within the lobby, which quickly shrank to silence as people turned to listen to the hotel manager. "Thank you. My colleague Mr Johnson and I have been discussing the situation with our guest Mr Hannigan here, who, as you may be aware, has seen the situation outside for himself. We wanted to give you an update. Mr Hannigan tells us that the situation outside is very serious, but we have no reason to believe that we ourselves are in any immediate danger in the hotel. We continue to believe that the best course of action is for us all to remain here and continue to support each other, as we are doing. We will have to see how the situation unfolds but for now, our advice is that we are safest if we all stay here. Thank you."

There was silence for a moment, then Colin shouted out, "Is that it? Is that the extent of the update? You need to tell us what's going on!"

Johnson spoke up. "As Mr Chung has said, we believe that the safest option is for us all to remain here, inside the hotel."

Colin persisted. "Yeah, that's all very well, but what aren't you telling us? You…" he gestured at Hannigan, "… can you tell us what you've seen?"

Hannigan went to speak, but Johnson cut across him. "Mr Hannigan has been in discussion with us, and we believe…"

"Yeah, we know," shouted Graham, "We need to remain here, but you need to tell us, what's going on out there?"

Johnson went to respond but was interrupted by a coldly calm voice from the back of the lobby. "That's exactly what I've been asking."

Heads swung around. Rob Mitchell had just walked out of the manager's office and was now standing with his hands on his hips at the back of the crowd. Now he walked through the small groups of people dotted across the lobby, and once more approached Johnson. "So you cut me off once, but now I think it's plain to see, these people…" he gestured airily behind him "… want an answer and they deserve an answer. What. Is. Going. On?"

Johnson and Chung exchanged helpless glances. Steve Hannigan stepped forward. "It's a fair point, you all have a right to know what's happening." The words sounded ominous, and the room fell silent. "It's bad out there, very bad. We think the battle is going to develop in the area around this hotel. It's very close now, and we need to be prepared for the fact that things might get worse."

There were some gasps and Gaby burst into tears. The lobby broke up into several disjointed but loud conversations. Tony Johnson shook his head bitterly and turned to Rob Mitchell, "This is exactly why we wanted to control the flow of information," he hissed, "Look at them. People are scared shitless."

"But at least they know," said Mitchell. "The worst thing of all is the fear of the unknown. And to answer your earlier question, *Mister* Johnson," he virtually spat the words with contempt, "on my Airbus, the passengers would now know that we were an engine down but that the highly skilled crew was doing everything in its power to resolve the situation. And at the risk of repeating myself, *at least they'd know.* Trying to keep information from people is unforgivable."

Johnson was puce; Mitchell turned away and spoke up, "Can I please ask my team to gather over here? Sarah, Dana, Rachel? Over here please. Ryan and Nigel still upstairs? OK, you three then please."

The three crew members moved across to join him, Rachel leaving Geddes in order to do so. Mitchell led them off to one side of the lobby. Dana thought that Rob suddenly seemed animated in a way he hadn't all night. "OK," he said, "I think that it's fairly clear now that these hotel types are not up to handling this kind of high pressure situation. People are worried, which is natural, but now they're also getting pissed off. I think we need to take charge of the situation. We've all had training. We know how to handle volatile situations."

"Yes, on aircraft," said Sarah, "but not in this kind of situation."

"Look at them," said Rob, casting his arm across the sweep of the lobby, "they're terrified. And ask yourself this – who in this lobby is trained specifically to deal with terrified people? Which group of people has the natural authority to lead in that kind of situation?"

Rachel was nodding along with him. "It's us, isn't it?" finished Rob. "A flight crew is the natural leadership group here. We take our training and we apply it to this situation. With the best will in the world, we are far better equipped to deal with this situation than a hotel manager and some guy whose day job is chucking out drunks from the bar."

He looked across at the rest of his crew. Rachel was still nodding. Sarah, arms folded, was silent but listening intently. He could tell that she was considering carefully what he had said. He looked across at Dana. Her face was inscrutable. He spoke up again, this time the questioning tone was gone from his voice and it was more authoritative.

"We need to take charge of this situation."

Across the lobby, Colin and Graham were looking across at the flight crew. "What's going on over there?" asked Graham.

Colin considered the scene for a moment. Memories of Board Room tactical plays and one-upmanship flashed into his mind. "Looks pretty much like a power grab to me," he said.

Lights Out

Tricia was consoling Gaby, wrapping her in both her arms in a veritable bear hug, but her daughter was still shaking as she sobbed. "Sweetheart, sweetheart, come on, it'll be OK."

"You don't know that," Gaby gasped between sobs, "You can't know that. We're all going to die, and that's that!"

Greta stepped forward. "Gaby, I'm sure that won't happen."

Gaby pulled out of her mother's embrace and pointed across the lobby to where Dave Geddes remained propped up against the wall on his makeshift bed. His eyes were closed and, even from this distance, he looked gravely ill. "Well, try telling that to *him*!"

Tricia closed her eyes. No fourteen-year old should have to deal with this. It was understandable that Gaby would be upset and disturbed by the scenes that she was witnessing, but she needed to try and keep her daughter calm. She walked back over to her and draped an arm across her shoulder. "He was just unlucky, Gaby, but he's got every chance of making it, thanks to the great work that *she* did." Tricia gestured across towards Dana, who was standing alongside some of the rest of her flight crew; they appeared to be in deep discussion.

Gaby looked across and suddenly burst into tears again. Her shoulders convulsed with great, wracking sobs, and Tricia was able to guide her gently into a corner. Gaby's crying was distressing for her to witness, but it was better, and more controllable, than her anger. Graham looked up and started across towards them, but Tricia, giving him a quick, tight, smile, held up her palm to hold him off. Graham got the message and returned to stand with Colin. He meant well, Tricia knew, but his trying to get involved would just be an extra complication for Gaby, and that was one thing that she *really* didn't need right now.

She rocked her daughter gently, and her mind went back well over a decade. She was sitting on a rug on a beach. The sun was riding high in a brilliant blue sky and the air was thick with a warm, dry heat. They were shaded by an olive tree, their backs to a small stone wall immediately behind them. It was cool under the cover of the dry leaves, which rustled and whispered in a gentle breeze which brought the faint scent of barbecuing meat. Tricia could taste a salty tang in the air. Gaby had fallen asleep in her arms; her tears were over now and she looked peaceful as she dozed. She had hurt herself jumping from the little wall and had been extremely upset only a few minutes ago, but now she slept, apparently without a care in the world. Tricia stroked her daughter's fine, blonde hair, and then moved a strand of her own, darker, hair away from her mouth, where the breeze had blown it. She looked out across the beach, down to where the waves were gently lapping up against the sand. The rhythmic washing noises were hypnotic and made her feel pleasantly drowsy. Just beyond the waves in waist deep water, Pete was wading out of the sea, back towards the beach after returning from his swim. Tricia looked from her daughter to her husband and back again. She felt a great contentment; she couldn't ever remember being this happy before, and she couldn't imagine how she could be any happier. Life was perfect.

Without any warning, the lights went out, plunging the lobby into darkness. There was a collective gasp from across the room, and several screams. Tricia realised that a background hum, that she hadn't previously been aware of, had stopped. The moon cast a silvery sheen through the top of the glass entrance doors where the piled-up furniture didn't quite reach meaning that although there was no lighting, the lobby was illuminated by a ghostly glow reflecting from its marble walls and floor. Gaby cried out and pulled away from Tricia, "Oh my god, what's happening?"

"It'll be OK, sweetheart, you'll see," Tricia soothed, but she heard the tremor in her own voice. Gaby's sobs started up again.

A male voice, commanding and tinged with a hint of an Essex accent, came across the lobby, "Please remain calm. There is no need for panic. We thought that this might happen."

A different male voice, cold and authoritative, also rang out, "Stay where you are. Don't move. Moving around in the dark could be dangerous."

The first voice again, "This is Tony Johnson, Head of Security for the hotel. That advice is correct. Please remain where you are. We have emergency lighting and we will get that activated now."

A torch clicked on, and the light from it danced on the floor as the person wielding it hurried across the lobby. The circle of bobbing light, along with some accompanying footsteps, disappeared down the steps at the far end of the great expanse.

There was very little movement within the lobby; people seemed to be heeding the twin pieces of advice they'd been given. The ghost light within pulsed as external flashes went off in the streets outside the hotel. In the relative silence, the noise of the mob outside could be clearly heard. There was a loud bang which made Tricia jump. She could hear screams and shots. It brought home to her just how close the fighting now was. She shivered and hoped that Gaby's sobs were helping to screen her from the noise.

Suddenly, a hum started up and a small number of emergency lights came on. In addition, about a quarter of the main lights were illuminated once more. There was the noise of footsteps on the stairs, and Tony Johnson came into view. "OK," he called, "That's the emergency generator started up. We should be OK now for lighting for several hours."

"That's if we make it that far," came a voice.

Tricia was continuing to soothe Gaby. She didn't know who had made that last, fatuous, remark but she desperately hoped her daughter had not heard it. She stroked Gaby's hair and rocked her gently, feeling the girl's broken sobs as though they were her own.

Relocation

They'd been hearing shots and explosions for many hours now, but nothing like this; the space right outside the hotel was suddenly alive with flashes, firing and huge bangs. The walls and doors shook repeatedly, and Dana could feel the floor vibrating beneath her. She glanced around; the guests in the lobby looked terrified, and she couldn't blame them; she felt a cold well of fear herself, but over the years she had perfected the art of acting with casual indifference. It had served her well, and she deployed her skills now as she sat beside Dave Geddes, holding one of his hands in hers. On his other side, Dana could see that Rachel was visibly frightened, but to her credit, she continued to sit in the place that she had adopted alongside him almost an hour ago.

Dana looked across. "Sounds real close now, Rach."

Rachel nodded mutely, staring dead ahead. Another huge explosion went off outside, and she flinched.

Tony Johnson approached. "How's he doing?"

"Not good," said Dana, "He's really struggling to breathe. He's not been conscious now for hours."

A wince passed across Johnson's features, and he seemed to consider his words carefully for a moment. "I'm going to suggest that everyone relocates to the restaurant they're building on the fifth floor of the tower. It's not finished but it's big enough to take everyone, and we'll be less exposed than we are down here."

"OK." Dana nodded, "Sounds like a plan."

"It's just…" Johnson nodded towards Geddes, propped up and looking sicker than anyone he had seen since the Falklands.

"We can't move him," said Dana, matter-of-factly.

"That's what I thought," said Johnson. He looked down at the floor. "So…" Another bang outside, and the sound of falling masonry.

"I'm gonna stay with him," said Dana in a matter-of-fact voice.

"Are you sure? That's risky. Maybe it would be better…"

"I can't leave him, Tony. Not like this."

Rachel spoke. "I'll stay too."

Steve Hannigan, who had been hovering on the fringes of the discussion spoke up in his baritone. "No, that's my job. You've done a wonderful job here, but he's my responsibility. I'll stay."

He looked at Dana. "I can stay with him on my own."

Dana smiled and wagged her index finger at him. "Ah-ah. That ain't gonna happen, mister. Gonna be Americans together on this one."

For a moment, she thought Hannigan was going to cry, then he said, simply, "Thank you."

Johnson walked away, into the middle of the lobby and clapped his hands. "Ladies and gentlemen, please can I have your attention? Due to the situation, we are going to relocate to the fifth floor of the tower. We'll be more sheltered there. Everybody, over to the stairs please. Move carefully and in an orderly way. There is no need to rush." People across the lobby started to get to their feet, Rachel amongst them. She looked down at Dana, "Be careful, Dana. Look after yourself. Look after him."

"See ya on the other side," said Dana.

Dana watched Rachel move towards the group of people starting to congregate around Tony Johnson but then she saw Rob Mitchell stride purposefully across to the Head of Security.

"Just a minute, Johnson," she heard him say.

Tony Johnson turned around and looked impassively at the airline captain. "Yes?"

Mitchell looked up at the taller man but he was unflinching as he spoke. "You're suggesting that we take everyone up there… up to a construction site?"

Johnson regarded him with cool hostility for a moment, then said, "It will be safer there than down here."

"It's a bloody building site, for God's sake!"

"I'm aware of that, Rob."

"We can't take people up there!"

"What else do you suggest? Haven't you heard what's going on out there?" Johnson gestured towards the barricade in front of the hotel doors.

Mitchell ignored the question. "Is there even an emergency plan for that part of the hotel? I bet there isn't."

Now it was Johnson's turn to ignore a question. "We don't have any alternative."

Around the two men, the other hotel guests had quietened and were watching the exchange in fascinated silence.

Mitchell spoke quietly but with purpose. "Oh, I think we do. I'm not prepared to take my chances in a half-built death trap on the fifth floor."

Johnson was white with anger. "What do you suggest Rob?" he hissed.

"I'm saying that we're in the process of being surrounded. It might be time for us to get out, now – while we still can."

Steve Hannigan spoke up. "You gotta be kiddin', man. It's like hell out there. Bein' on the streets ain't no place to be – no way. We wouldn't stand a chance."

Mitchell stiffened. "So maybe staying put in a shell of a building and waiting to be overwhelmed by these – forces - isn't exactly the smartest thing to do. We need to make preparations to evacuate. We need to get out of here whilst we still can."

Tony Johnson raised his palms, "Rob, nobody is going anywhere. It's far too dangerous. We stay here, we wait it out."

Mitchell turned to him, "On exactly whose authority are you acting?"

"On mine," said Lee Chung, from behind Tony Johnson. "The safety of everybody in this hotel is my responsibility, and I trust Mr Johnson here to make the correct decisions that will keep everybody safe."

"Well, I'm saying he's called this wrong," said Mitchell.

A woman's voice came from within the crowd in the lobby, "What did you mean when you said we're being surrounded?"

Mitchell shot a swift glance at Johnson and then looked back at the woman who had asked the question. "Exactly what I said, Madam. The battle is moving down towards the hotel. It's virtually outside already – you must have heard it. This part of the city is a dead end. The battle is going to be fought right outside, and I say we leave – now – whilst we all still have a chance."

There were gasps and mutterings from across the lobby. Lee Chung spoke up, above the noise, "Mr Mitchell! I counsel you to please stop this agitation. We take our lead from Mr Johnson, and we will heed his advice."

Mitchell spun around, "I'm sorry, Mr Chung. I've enjoyed staying here over the years; it's a good hotel and you're a good manager. And a good man. But I cannot stand by whilst we let ourselves be overrun by what is now effectively a civil war. We have to leave, and we have to do it now. My flight crew and I will be leaving, and we will gladly escort any other guests who want to come with us. But we will be leaving immediately."

The noise within the lobby was now rising to a crescendo. "Don't do this Rob," shouted Tony Johnson, "You've no idea what it's like out there; you're not equipped for this." He turned to the guests in the lobby and addressed them beseechingly, "Please, listen to me. It's really for the best if you stay in the hotel. Yes, we expect it will become violent, but there are places to hide, to shelter in here. We can ride it out. Please, please, do not take your chances on the street."

Rob Mitchell shouted out again, "My crew and I are leaving right now. You can make your choice to come with us or stay here."

Dana looked up from her position at Geddes' side. "I'm not going," she said softly, "I can't leave him."

Mitchell stiffened and looked down at her. "I would strongly advise..."

But Dana cut him off. "It's my final decision," she said firmly. "*My* decision."

"Your choice," snapped Mitchell and turned abruptly on his heel. He beckoned to Sarah, Rachel and the male flight attendants, who had joined the others, to follow him. Rachel looked stricken. Her eyes darted from Johnson to Mitchell and back again. She seemed to reach a decision and moved into place behind the airline captain.

A loud explosion detonated outside and there was the sound of falling masonry. Tricia felt panicked by choice, and by events. She looked wildly around her. Within the strange mixture of emergency lighting and subdued main lighting, the people in the lobby looked like spectres, hovering in the shadows, but their silhouettes seeming to loom grotesquely out of them.

Gaby started to wail, "I need to leave, I need to leave!"

Tricia bit down on the bile forming in her own throat and swallowed hard, "Shush, baby, shush."

Her daughter was hyperventilating now, "Got to get out, got to get out!"

Around them, other guests were experiencing similar paroxysms of anxiety. Out of the corner of her eye, Tricia could see the airline captain starting to move through to the bar which she knew contained a rear entrance. In anguish, she looked across at Graham. Her husband was standing next to his brother, still slack-jawed at the shouted discussion which had just taken place in front of them. She caught his eye. He looked directly at her, and the phrase "rabbit in the headlights" had never been more apt. Tricia looked back at Gaby, who was now bent over double, one arm sticking out at a right angle and holding the wall. Her long, blonde hair cascaded towards the floor and she stood there, heaving both with sobs and snatched breaths. In an instant, Tricia's mind was made up. "Graham, we need to go. We need to get her out of here. We need to go. With him." She pointed towards Rob Mitchell who was now moving purposefully towards the bar area, one of the flight attendants at his shoulder, the female co-pilot just behind her, and a number of other guests trailing in their wake.

On the other side of the lobby, other guests were starting to climb the stairs, as Tony Johnson started to shepherd people up towards the tower.

As the two groups started to diverge, Graham looked panicked. Tricia saw Colin lean in close to him and say something. Her husband nodded, and the two men tapped each other on the back. Then Graham came across, looking pale and drawn. "OK," he said simply.

By unspoken agreement, each of them went to either side of Gaby and placed a supportive arm around her. Then, with their daughter sobbing and retching between them, they helped her to join the small exodus leaving the hotel.

__Americans__

Hannigan watched them go, shaking his head. For Christ's sake, did these people not understand? Outside was a fucking warzone, these civilians wouldn't stand a chance out there; it had been bad enough for people like him and Geddes, who'd been there before. The thought of his colleague brought his mind back into focus, and he looked down at the cameraman.

It seemed that the makeshift bandage and wraparound tourniquet that the flight attendant had applied were doing their job; he couldn't see any sign of leaking blood. Geddes' face was a deathly shade of grey, his breathing often shallow but occasionally rasping. Beads of sweat stood out on his forehead like a row of marbles waiting to be flicked. His arms lay limply by his sides.

Hannigan squatted, easing his bulk into position with a grunt. He looked at the flight attendant. "Thank you," he said.

Dana looked up from administering a cold compress to Geddes' cheek, "You already said that." She smiled, "All part of the service."

"My god, you're an angel."

Dana shrugged. "I very much doubt *that*."

Hannigan gave a humourless laugh. "That may be so, but you may have saved my buddy's life here."

There was silence whilst Dana administered to her patient again.

"And you're an American," said Hannigan. "Deep South?"

"Texas," said Dana, "Lubbock. I'm Dana."

"Steve."

"I've seen ya on the TV."

Hannigan grunted, "Occupational hazard. I guess most of my earlier assignments have been more successful than this one."

"How so?"

"Oh, you know… bein' there at the start of the trouble, staying there whilst it unfolds, not gettin' shot, not losin' the fucking camera. Just shit like that."

Dana snorted and then held up a hand to her mouth. "I'm sorry, Steve, that just sounds funny. I know it shouldn't, but it does." She seemed to be choking behind her hand.

"Yeah, well, when you put it like that…" Hannigan also started to chuckle, a deep rumble making its way up from his diaphragm, until he could no longer hold it in and he burst out laughing. Dana lost all pretence and also let forth a gale of laughter, spitting out saliva from behind the back of her hand as she did so.

For a few seconds, they rocked together in mirth, their laughter echoing off the marble walls of the lobby. Most of the remaining guests looked across at them, wondering what was going on; wondering what could possibly be so funny in the midst of such an unprecedented emergency? In less than a minute their laughter subsided and they both looked at Geddes' pale face, almost as one. It was a sobering sight.

Hannigan wiped his eyes, looked up and focused on Geddes. "Jesus," he said, "what a mess."

"A-men to that," said Dana, who was once more applying the compress.

Hannigan looked across towards the bar area. He tilted his head, "You didn't want to go with them?"

Dana shook her head. "Nah. I'm needed here. Plus, I didn't wanna take my chances out there."

Hannigan nodded, then asked, "But isn't that captain your boss?"

Dana smiled, "On this trip, yeah. And under normal circumstances, yeah. But are you callin' these normal circumstances?" Her smile turned into a grin.

Hannigan was silent for a moment, and then spoke. "Well, I'm glad you're here," he said. He'd wanted to say more.

Convoy

Rob strode out into the bar area, aware that he had a significant number of people following him. On the periphery of his senses, he became aware of flashes and explosions going off outside the hotel. They sounded closer than ever. As his little caravan moved through the bar, he caught a sight of it in a mirror that they passed; Rachel directly behind him, Sarah following, head down; behind her, a thin stream of people, all looking haggard, pale, and most of all, worried.

He moved past the bar's counter and into the small ante room that an hour earlier, he'd been in as he'd helped drag in Dave Geddes from the street. A couple of silver beer kegs were in the way of the door. He bent to try and move the first of them out of the way and then became aware of a body shoving itself through the small crowd to join him. Rob looked around; it was the guest who'd helped him bring Geddes through earlier, the chubby, balding one. The pilot grunted a "Thanks," as both men hauled the first barrel out of the way and then did the same with the second barrel. Rob unlocked the door and drew back the two bolts at its top and bottom. He tried the handle of the door that led to the outside; it wouldn't open. He tried again, with the same negative result. Now, he pressed down whilst also putting his shoulder to it; the door burst open and suddenly, he could see the alleyway beyond.

It was the same alleyway that he'd seen only an hour or so earlier, but now it seemed different; then it had been a small, dark passageway, but now, although its dimensions were clearly the same, it seemed somehow larger, wider. The pulsing light of nearby fires lit the alleyway and regular flashes illuminated it still further, whilst the noise of the battle raging only a couple of blocks away seemed to fill the space and reverberated between the walls on either side of the alley. For a moment he paused in the doorway, unsure whether he was doing the right thing. Then he looked over his shoulder at the guests who were now following him, *relying* on him, and he took a deep breath and assessed his options. His instincts told him that they should go left; earlier that evening he had run to the right to help recover Geddes, and that had taken them to the front of the hotel. That seemed to be where most of the sounds of fighting were coming from, and he wanted to get as far away from that as possible.

In his mind, he saw the map on the wall of Lee Chung's office once more. He knew that the streets would be no-go zones; he was relying on alleyways and footpaths to get his little group to safety. He was sure that if only they could break out of the downtown area containing the hotel, they would be free of the major scene of the battle. Surely other areas of the city must be safer? Maybe there was no violence in other areas at all; he had to hope so – with no communication available, anything that was happening anywhere else in the city was a guessing game.

Still standing in the open doorway, one hand resting lightly on each frame, he was about to move out into the alley when he heard his name called. He looked over his shoulder, saw Rachel and was reassured, but then he saw Sarah Booth, head down and knew instantly that it was she who had called out for him. He snapped his head around. "What?"

Sarah's head remained down. He found himself looking directly at the crown of her head. "I'm… I'm not coming."

"What?"

"I don't think it's right. I think the best thing to do is to stay put and wait it out. I'm… sorry."

"Sarah, wait…"

"I'm sorry Rob, I'm going back to help Dana."

"Dana?" He swore under his breath, "Fuck."

Out of the corner of his eye, he saw his First Officer moving back, past the line of distressed guests, through the ante room and towards the main body of the hotel. He went to call after her, but his voice caught in his throat and seeing the queue of expectant followers, he thought better of it. Instead, he glanced quickly to the woman immediately behind him. "You still with me?" he asked.

"I'm still here, Rob," said Rachel. But she sounded oddly quiet.

Rob Mitchell took a deep breath and stepped out into the alleyway. "OK, this way," he shouted, "We're heading left!"

An Awkward Moment

"What did you say to him?" asked Greta. Colin watched the last of the ten or so guests who were leaving disappear into the bar area and then turned to his wife. "I told him that I thought he was making a mistake. That they'd be better off here. But... that in the end he had to do what was right for him and his family."

"Where will they go?"

"No idea, and I don't think the pilot does either."

"Do you think they'll be OK?"

"I hope so."

"But do you think they will?"

Colin bit down on his lip. He shook his head. "I just don't know, Greta. I really don't."

In that moment, Greta thought that he looked like a little boy lost. She touched his forearm gently and he gave her a weak smile in return. Then she saw his smile broaden. She turned around to see what had caused his apparent lift in mood and saw the female First Officer walking back into the lobby. Greta felt a cold shiver run through her. She saw Colin look away quickly, towards the other side of the lobby, and she saw the colour rising in his cheeks. She felt distant and sad.

Colin looked back again. "I'm sure they'll be fine," he said, with what was clearly a forced level of conviction. Greta nodded. She felt like she might cry. Looking up, she saw people moving slowly up the stairs. It gave her a legitimate excuse to move away for a few moments and collect herself, she thought. "I'm going up into the tower," she said, her back to Colin. He was about to reply, but she was already moving away from him. "I'll come up too," he called after her, lamely. She either didn't hear him or ignored him. He dug his hands into his pockets and sighed.

"Hey, you OK?" Sarah asked.

"I – I'm just worried about Graham and his family, about all of them in fact."

"I know. Hell of a decision to take."

"But you came back."

She wasn't sure whether it was a question or a statement, but she answered it anyway.

"I initially thought I'd go from a sense of loyalty, but I don't think – in fact, I'm sure – that Rob has got a plan. He just wants to be in charge; he can't bear to see somebody else leading. So when it came to the crunch, it just didn't seem like the right thing to do. All my instincts were telling me that I should be here." She looked across to Dana, who was taking Dave Geddes' pulse. "And I didn't want to leave Dana on her own. Well, not on her own, but you know..." She trailed off.

"I'm glad you came back," said Colin quietly.

There was a pause and then Sarah said, "We actually need to barricade that door again, if you want to give me a hand?"

"Sure."

Sarah led the way back through the empty bar, and into the small ante room, Colin following her. The key was still in the door, and Sarah turned it, then drew across bolts at the top and bottom. The beer kegs were off to one side of the door, where they'd been heaved across by Rob Mitchell and Graham Brazier. Sarah bent to the first one and prepared to push it into position. She waited for a second and then Colin joined her, standing opposite. He braced himself against the keg and looked up, directly at Sarah. Their eyes locked. For a moment he considered leaning over and kissing her; the image sprang very clearly into his mind. Then Sarah said, "OK, ready?" and the moment was gone.

They pushed the keg into place and then did the same with the second one. "That's a bit of peace of mind," said Sarah.

"Yep." Colin avoided her gaze but Sarah didn't notice. She was dusting off her hands as she walked back out into the bar area. Colin wiped his own hands on his trousers and followed her. He couldn't decide whether he'd missed an opportunity or dodged a bullet.

Alleyway

The alleyway was dark but illuminated sporadically by the flashes and flares of the pitched battle taking place a couple of blocks away. Rob led the way, keeping to the side of the hotel and proceeding in a crouch. Rachel was behind him and, turning, he could see a thin line of ten or so guests following her. The teenage girl was there, stumbling along in between her parents, apparently in a daze. Rob faced back in the direction they were heading. Up ahead, he could see where the alley came to an end, where a low wall cut across the path.

A loud explosion rocked the air somewhere behind them and Rob flinched. Somebody in the group behind him let out a yelp. He heard a whispered, "Oh my god!" He stopped his advance and turned around, holding up his palms and then pushing them down in a quietening gesture, and then continued with his stealthy creep forwards. He reached the wall. It was about four feet in height and made of concrete. White paint peeled from its sides. It was more of a delineation than a physical boundary and he peered over it. Beyond was a wide footpath leading through some trees and beyond that, the sea. There were streetlamps along the route of the pathway, but they were all dark. The moon was bright and almost overhead though, allowing him to see reasonably well. The trees swayed slightly in the light breeze coming from the sea. The scene ahead of him seemed peaceful and utterly incompatible with the chaotic noises which were still rumbling behind him.

He hoisted himself up onto the wall and over onto the other side. His feet landed on springy grass. "OK," he hissed back over the wall, "Come on over." Rachel levered herself over the wall and dropped alongside him. One by one the others followed, some being helped over. Within a minute or so, everyone was over.

Graham Brazier crept up to Rob. "What now?" he whispered.

"We head that way," said Rob gesturing along the path in the direction that led away from the street battle.

"Where does it go?"

"Not sure, but it should get us away from here. We can get clear, find somewhere to lay up, just away from all of this."

Graham nodded and turned to check on Tricia and Gaby, giving them a double thumbs up.

"OK," hissed Rob, "let's go." A plan was forming in his mind. This wide, meandering path looked like it would be a favourite for joggers and roller bladers. There were trails like this in coastal cities the world over, often running along the sea front for several miles. He thought this one would be much the same, and if it was, a couple of miles should get them well clear of this area, and it shouldn't take more than half an hour or so. He thought about the others in the hotel, waiting for their fate like rats in a cage. He imagined his return to the UK; he'd be a national hero, his leadership capabilities on display for all to see. Surely Harriet would forgive him then? She was as ambitious as he was, and she wouldn't be able to let an opportunity like this slip through her fingers. He imagined being back in the house with Harriet and the girls; it was a feeling that was almost tangible. He hadn't exactly planned it this way, but this civil disorder was going to work out pretty well for him, he was sure. He heard Rachel rustling along behind him and he smiled to himself; she was bound to be very grateful to him for getting her out of the hotel in one piece. His imagination wandered from the house in Surrey to what sort of reward Rachel was likely to give him. A brief image of Dana flashed into his mind, and he dismissed it. As far as he was concerned, she was history now.

Under the moonlight, the thin line of former hotel guests wound its way through the trees.

Despair

"What the…" Emerging from the trees, Rob was dismayed to see that the path had run out and not just the path but the rest of the land, too. What Rob had expected to be a long coastal path had turned out to be a shortcut through a small copse to the waterfront. He was standing on an exposed, grassy, promontory. Waves lapped on three sides with the trees behind them the only way back to dry land. It was a dead end. Rachel came up behind him. "Shit, no," she breathed, aghast. Now others were joining them, and gasps of despair echoed around the small group.

"What the hell do we do now?" somebody shouted.

"We keep our frigging voices down for a start!" hissed Graham Brazier, and Rob was grateful to him for his intercession.

"He's right," added Rob in an undertone. "We need to keep quiet and keep calm. And we need to retrace our steps."

There was a groan. Rob spoke again. "We go back down this path, back through the trees, we go past the little wall and we find another alley or side street to cut down, then we head back in this direction. There must be some kind of path that leads us along the sea front."

In front of him, the teenage girl had her face in her hands. Rob could see her shoulders starting to shake. Her mother tried to comfort her. "Gaby, sweetheart…"

Time for some authoritative advice, thought Rob. He stepped forward. "Gaby, listen to me please." He knew that his voice had a calm resonance; it had worked its magic on countless flights when issues presented themselves. He saw the girl's demeanour change slightly; she had tilted her head to listen. "We have to do this," he murmured. "We have to. We all have to be brave for each other, and we've just got to go a little way down there, and then we can turn around again. It will only take us a few minutes, but we have to be brave in that time. Can you do that, Gaby?"

Gaby nodded. "Good girl. OK, let's go."

He pushed back through the small crowd so that he was once more leading, and then set off back through the trees. Rachel fell back this time, so that the Brazier family, and in particular Gaby, could follow the pilot directly. They passed the small wall that they'd clambered over only minutes earlier. Briefly, Rob considered whether they should go back that way, but that felt like admitting defeat, and he pressed on.

There were buildings around them again now, and they stayed pressed against the wall of the nearest one. It could have been the hotel; Rob wasn't sure, he was starting to lose his bearings. Keeping his hand against the brick, he advanced slowly and carefully. He came to a corner, where a small side street cut across their path. They were moving directly towards where the loudest noises were coming from, and it was an unnerving feeling. He just prayed that this latest plan worked better than the last one. He stopped at the corner and, taking great care, peered around. The street was empty save for some parked cars. They looked undamaged in the moonlight and the buildings around looked safe and intact. Were it not for the flashes and bangs erupting from the immediate vicinity, this could just be any other early morning in this part of the city, Rob thought. He looked around; his followers were bunched up immediately behind him. All on me, he thought, all on me.

He inched himself around the corner and onto the side street proper, once more moving along the side of the building. Behind him, the others were doing the same. In his peripheral vision, he saw Gaby creep out and around the corner, her step-father following her. Rob was crouching low now, moving very stealthily; every footstep a cautious one. Ahead, he could see a small crossroads where yet another side street intersected. He felt relief. Once they reached the junction, they could turn down the street and they would once more be heading in the right direction, and away from the mayhem.

He felt his spirits start to lift and began to feel that they would be alright.

And then the air was torn apart by a burst of automatic gunfire. He saw it a split second before he heard it, a jagged sparkle of yellow fire rippling from a building on the other side of the street, and then the sound came, thunderous and devastating. Rob immediately sprinted as fast as he could towards the crossroads ahead of him. Behind him, Gaby screamed. She stood, immobile as her scream echoed off the surrounding buildings. Tricia, just rounding the corner, froze in position and the people behind her stopped abruptly. Other than Rob, the only person who moved was Graham Brazier. He launched himself at Gaby with a speed that belied his paunch, and knocked her to the ground, where he spread himself across her as best he could, splaying his arms and legs in the process. There was another burst of fire, and suddenly Graham's body was jerking crazily. A fountain of blood sprayed against the wall of the building that they were lying against. Tricia, watching horrified from the street corner, screamed. Graham's torso jerked again. The gunfire stopped. Blood flowed copiously across the pavement. Graham lay still. Beneath his body, there was movement. Gaby wriggled out from underneath him and fled to her mother, who still stood at the corner, screaming. The gunfire came again, but Gaby reached the corner and the relative safety of the side street. Somebody pulled Tricia back the same way so that she was no longer exposed.

Rob Mitchell had made it to the crossroads. He ducked down the street and then carefully looked around the corner to see what had happened. He saw Graham Brazier's body, lying immobile. It was dark and the body was several scores of metres away, but even so, Mitchell could see that half of Graham's face had been shot away. Rob Mitchell swallowed hard and then, alone, started to run down the side street that he now found himself on. As he ran, the sounds of Tricia Brazier's continuing screams overlaid the noise of the battle.

Stand-off

Johnson stepped across to the windows of the restaurant and carefully looked out. Below him, he could see a stand-off developing. In the street, a row of armoured personnel carriers formed a formidable shield for the personnel massing behind them. He noted that the security forces now seemed to be purely formed of individuals wearing khaki; whether this meant that they were all army, or whether some of the police were now re-clothed, he wasn't sure. Facing against the APCs was a surging but motley mob of civilians. Looking down he could see masked protesters, amongst the general mass of people. He spotted people holding what looked like makeshift clubs, and caught the glint of moonlight on glass – petrol bombs, he thought. He had no doubt that there were also more than a few rifles, pistols and maybe even automatic weapons down there.

He'd suspected that this would happen from the moment that he and Lee Chung had reviewed the wall map, with the help of Steve Hannigan's eye witness intelligence. He'd been sure that the battle would come to them, that the denouement would occur right outside the hotel. And now he'd been proved right. He just prayed that his other instinct, that to stay put rather than flee, was also correct.

Lee Chung joined him at the window. "So… this is it, Tony. This is the endgame."

Keeping his eyes fixed on the scene in the street, Tony nodded. "I think so. This is it. They have nowhere else to push them to. Over there…" he pointed to a dark area beyond the hotel, "… is just trees and then a small bit of land jutting out into the sea. They're cornered. They either stand and fight now, or they surrender."

Below them, a flame flared, and then another, and another. "There go the petrol bombs," said Johnson. Shots were fired and the crowd howled. A wave of noise cascaded up from the street below, washing off the walls five stories below them and then rattling the windows.

Lee Chung peered down. "It looks like they are making a fight of it," he said, grimly.

Now the crowd was surging and battling. The shooting and the noise intensified. The sound of breaking glass came from the street level.

Johnson moved away from the windows, and pulled Lee Chung with him. "Time to get away from these windows and batten down the hatches," he said. Lee Chung went to the restaurant door, pushed it to and locked it. Several guests then joined Johnson in moving some tables and chairs into position behind it to form another barricade. Once that was done, he turned to the people in the room, "OK, please remain calm; we may be here for some time. I suggest that we sit against that wall over there, away from the windows and the door." He gestured to the wall on the far side of the restaurant, and the guests in the room dutifully filed over to it.

Colin saw that Greta had chosen a spot towards one end of the wall, and he went to sit next to her. She saw him approach, then stood up and moved to the opposite side. Colin felt hi stomach lurch and colour rise in his cheeks; he carried on and sat down where he had been planning to, with Greta now several feet away to his left. He saw Sarah coming across and tried to avoid eye contact. Part of him hoped that she'd sit next to him, but an equal part hoped that she'd sit as far away as possible. She ended up positioning herself a few people to the right of Colin.

Johnson and Chung saw that everyone was settled and then came across and joined them. Sitting there in a row, all eyes on the empty bar opposite them at the far end of the restaurant, Johnson couldn't help feeling like they were helplessly awaiting a firing squad.

<u>Blame Game</u>

She could hear the noise outside intensifying; it sounded like the clashes were really violent out there now. Dana was grateful for the barricade across the main doors, but she wished that she could see through it so that she had a feel for what was going on outside. Then again, maybe she was better off not knowing…

"Fuckin' crazy out there now," said Hannigan.

"Sure sounds like it." She was doing her casually unaffected act again, but her stomach felt leaden, and her mouth was suddenly dry. She looked across at Dave Geddes, still propped between the two of them.

Hannigan seemed to read her mind. "This is bad news for Dave. He needed hospital treatment hours ago. Now…" his voice trailed off.

He didn't need to finish; she knew exactly what he meant – now, with a full blown street battle taking place outside, his chance was virtually gone.

She sighed, and stood up to stretch her legs and back. "Well Steve, you just never know. You just gotta keep hoping." But she knew that she was a long way from sounding convincing.

Hannigan looked at his colleague with something approaching affection. "He's a great guy Dana, he really is. He didn't deserve this. Maybe if we hadn't…"

"Hey!" Dana pulled him up sharply. "None of us deserved any of this, Kid. And you guys, well – you were just doing your job weren't you? Don't you go blaming yourself, now."

"No, you're right. Occupational hazard; I guess his luck just ran out tonight."

"I guess. But you did amazingly just to get him back here. If it wasn't for you, he'd have had no chance at all."

"Me and a coupla strangers. And you, of course. You got him this far, Dana."

For a moment, neither of them said anything, the sudden silence between them starkly countered by the grotesque sounds from outside. Dark thoughts clouded Hannigan's mind. There was an image that he couldn't get rid of. It was of their camera, bouncing and skittering across the road. All of that footage… the kind of footage that won awards… gone. He glanced back at his colleague and then hated himself for thinking about the camera at a time like this. But – did it mean that Geddes' suffering was all for nothing?

The silence stretched on. Eventually, it was Hannigan who punctured it. "So, I wonder how your guy is getting on with his breakaway group?"

"Rob?" Dana rolled her eyes, "Who knows?"

"Not a fan?"

Dana blew out her cheeks. "Rob is..." she searched for the words, "... someone who likes to take charge. Likes to *be* in charge. Actually, he *needs* to be in charge." She paused for a second, "OK, he's a control freak." She gave a brief, mirthless, laugh. "But," she said, "he's good, very good. If anyone can get those guys to safety, it's Rob, but he'll do it his way and nobody else's. I hope they're doing OK out there."

Hannigan nodded and then looked up at Dana. "What time is it?"

Dana checked her watch. "3am. Jeez, what a night. I sure as hell had other plans for this time of the night."

"Yeah? Like what?"

Dana arched an eyebrow. "Now that," she said, "would be tellin'."

Despite himself, Hannigan chuckled. "I get it," he said, "flight crew let off the leash and let loose, huh? I wondered why they called them layovers."

"And I bet reporters have plenty of moments too."

"OK, guilty as charged." Hannigan held up his hands. "I've had plenty of *moments*, as you call them. Most of us in this business have. It's the adrenaline, the danger. It courses through you and makes everything more – vivid. In those circumstances..." he broke off, remembering something, and a faint smile played across his lips. The smile, though, faded from his face as he looked once more at Geddes. "Poor bastard," he muttered.

Change of Plan

Tricia was continuing to scream. Gaby was doubled over, hands on her hips, gasping. Most of the other people who'd been in Rob Mitchell's breakaway party were pinned back against the wall, eyes wide, terror on their faces. Some people hissed "Shhhh..." towards Tricia, but most just held themselves back, rigid against the wall, and stood there, mute. Rachel was the only one to take any positive action. She quickly cast her eye over both Tricia and Gaby and, assessing that Tricia was the one in greater need of help, moved across to her. She put an arm round Tricia's shoulders and steered her towards the wall. Tricia continued to wail, but it was no longer the high pitched scream that it had been; it was more of a series of long, choking sobs. If anything, Rachel thought, it was worse.

"Gr... Graham, Graham, no... no, no..." Tricia was sobbing now, her hands held up to her face. She was sucking in great gulps of air between her sobs. Rachel held her, gripping her in a tight bear hug, patting the top of her back and whispering to her. They remained like that for a minute or so, in the most emotive embrace either of them had ever experienced, whilst Gaby remained bent double and the others remained in their terrified trances.

Another burst of gunfire. The sound of heavy vehicles on the move could be heard. They sounded close. Very close. Screams and shouts echoed down the street that they were on. Rachel continued to pat the top of Tricia's shoulders, but having got over the initial shock of what had just happened, she started to focus again. Nobody else seemed to realise the extreme danger that they were in, and she lifted her head. "Everyone," she called over Tricia's shoulder, "Everyone, listen, we need to move out of here. It isn't safe, we need to move back."

"Move back where?" somebody shouted.

Rachel thought for a moment. "Back to the hotel," she said.

There were groans. "No way!" "What?"

Rachel bridled. "Don't you realise? Didn't you see what just happened? We're not safe here. We have to get back to the hotel."

One of the other guests, a thin, angular man with greying brown hair, moved away from the wall and stood in front of her. "After everything that we've been through? Your captain promised us he'd get us out of this hell hole, and now one of us has been killed, and you're telling us that after all that, we just go back to where we started from? And what? Pretend that none of this ever happened?"

Rachel was rarely, if ever, roused to anger but now she turned to the man in a sudden fury. "Well, what do you suggest instead? Have you got a better idea? Let's hear it then! Otherwise, shut up!"

The angular man stepped backwards, shocked. Rachel had surprised herself with her sudden burst of anger, but it seemed to have worked. The others were silent; the only sounds to be heard, Tricia's wracking sobs and Gaby's continued gasps. Rachel glanced at the teenager; she literally hadn't said a word since her stepfather had flung himself on top of her and died in the process. Need to watch her, she thought.

Rachel looked around the small group. With her own eyes, she had seen Rob run off as she had pulled a screaming Tricia back around the corner. She knew he had gone; left them. Scanning the people in front of her now, she knew that it would be down to her to get them back; if left to their own devices, these people wouldn't be able to decide what to do between them. She stepped forward and took a deep breath. She had a sudden confidence, born of the conviction that what she was about to suggest was absolutely the right thing to do under the circumstances. "OK," she said in a calm but commanding voice, "We're doing it, we're going back to the hotel. Anyone who's with me, follow me. We're leaving, and we're leaving now."

She turned to Tricia, gripped her arm and started to pull her along with her, back down the side of the wall and in the direction from which they'd originally come. She looked over her shoulder and saw that Gaby, her clothes streaked and splashed with Graham's blood, was starting to follow, trailing along in her mother's wake, head down and still silent. Some of the others were starting to stir and were also following. Rachel turned her concentration back to their direction of travel. She was focused and purposeful; she had believed in Rob but he had let them down more than she could have believed. Now it was down to her, and she was determined that she would not fail her small cohort; she was going to lead them to the safety of the hotel.

Under a Blazing Sun

Dana leaned across Geddes and placed her cheek in front of his mouth and nose; she felt for his pulse. "Shit, Steve, we're losing him."

She immediately pulled Geddes into a prone position and started chest compressions, then moved to providing artificial respiration.

"Ah…" Hannigan sounded pained, himself, "God… what can I do?"

"Can you do the chest compressions? Know what to do?"

Hannigan nodded, "Yeah."

"OK, let's do that." Dana went back to breathing into Geddes' mouth.

Hannigan moved around, placed one palm laterally on top of the other and started rhythmically rocking onto his friend's chest. To his right, he was vaguely aware of Dana providing Geddes' breaths for him. Hannigan kept up his routine. He knew it might be hopeless, but he kept going, and he found the rocking rhythm strangely soothing and hypnotic.

His mind wandered from the here and now to a different time, a different place…

He and Geddes in a jeep, speeding along under a blazing sun, the wheels spraying up grit, the ribbon of black tarmac they were following barely visible under its dusting of sand. They were both laughing, exhilarated by their own survival. Hannigan, driving, stole a glance at Geddes, who patted the camera on his lap like a proud father. "All in the can!" he yelled above the noise of the jeep's engine. Hannigan whooped. They had some seriously good footage of the latest skirmish to take place in Mogadishu. The clashes they had just filmed had been brief but violent and they had managed to film the most important of the local warlords directing the men under his command. They had been spotted, been shot at and chased, but they had made it out of there and were virtually home and free now. Man, this felt good! He whooped again and floored the accelerator. The jeep sped through a dusty settlement; to call it a town would be stretching things. A few dilapidated buildings stood on either side of the parched road. A child in rags looked up to watch them pass, and no sooner had they reached the settlement than they were through it again, back out into the desert. They sped on, the jeep throwing up clouds of sand and dust. He felt grimy, he was covered in grit, dirt and his own sweat, but he was in his element. He looked across at Dave and knew that he felt the same.

A seemingly distant voice brought him back to the present.

"It's no use," said Dana, "I'm sorry, but he's gone."

Hannigan continued his compressions.

"It's been over ten minutes, Steve. I'm so sorry, but we've lost him." She knelt up and swept her long dark hair back over her head. Beads of sweat on her forehead were pushed into her hair too, and she felt a trickle of dampness run down the side of her cheek.

Hannigan rocked back against the wall and buried his face in his hands. "Oh Jesus, Jesus I'm sorry Dave, I'm sorry."

Dana padded across on her knees, beside Geddes' body and put her arms around Hannigan. "Not your fault, not your fault, not your fault." She murmured the words over and over, like a lullaby.

They remained there like that for several minutes; Hannigan slumped against the wall, Dana on her knees with her arms around him, awkwardly leaning in towards him, Geddes' body off to one side. Outside, the chaos and clamour continued.

Journey

It was only a journey of a few hundred metres, but it was the most stressful of Rachel's life, escorting the terrified people, clinging to the relative safety of the wall to their side, keeping one eye out for combatants, and the other on Tricia and Gaby. Her heart thudded like a quick drumbeat, her breaths coming in snatched gasps. She kept turning to check on Tricia and Gaby, both now staggering like zombies. Rachel thought that they both seemed to have zoned out; it was like they were on autopilot. She caught a glimpse of Tricia's hollow eyes, and it didn't seem like there was any life behind them. Behind Tricia, one of the other guests was helping Gaby stumble along.

Presently, they came to the small wall that marked the end of the alleyway running behind the hotel.

"OK," whispered Rachel, "Over we go. Almost there."

One by one, the guests clambered over the wall and dropped to the other side, some doing so on their own, others with the help of some of their colleagues. Rachel saw everyone over and then started to creep down the alleyway, checking over her shoulder to make sure that the others were following; they were. This was now familiar territory to her, and she started to, if not relax, at least feel a little more optimistic about the situation.

Suddenly, there was rapid movement off to her right hand side. She froze in position, terrified for what might appear, but it turned out to be a rat which was poking around on the periphery of the alleyway. It paused for a moment, sniffed the air cautiously and then scuttled off. Rachel realised she had been holding her breath; she exhaled loudly and continued to move forwards.

She continued to brush against the wall to her right; she was fairly convinced now that this was the hotel. Beyond, the noise of the battle was intense and deafening. Engines, shots, screams, sirens, shouts, glass breaking, explosions, helicopters – the wall of sound was almost overwhelming, but she hoped that all the combatants' focus was on that battle, and that nobody was watching their slow progress down the alley.

Time seemed to be running incredibly slowly but at last she came to the rear door that they'd exited an hour or so earlier. Feeling the first stirrings of relief, she grasped the handle and turned it. Locked. Her heart sank. Behind her, the others had caught her up and were now lined up alongside the wall. She could feel the tension in the air. Behind her, she could hear Tricia's teeth chattering. The night was balmy and warm and she knew without doubt that Tricia was shivering as shock started to set in. She tried the door handle again, but knew it was hopeless.

"What's going on?" somebody hissed.

"It's locked."

"Is there any other way in?"

"I don't know. The front is barricaded. I think it's just this entrance."

"What about where they receive their deliveries?" someone whispered.

"That must be round the front," she heard somebody answer, "where the main road is. Maybe there's a goods entrance. We could try that."

Rachel shook her head. "No way, that's far too dangerous. We can't risk going round there – that's where all the fighting's taking place."

She knocked at the door, lightly at first, but then with increasing force.

"Shhhhh!" somebody rasped from behind her.

"We've got no other choice!" snapped Rachel. "We've just got to pray that somebody hears us."

She started to beat the palm of her hand against the door. Somebody joined her and started to hammer on it with a fist. Rachel knew they were making a lot of noise, but she was past caring now. She was just desperate for somebody to hear them.

The Ante Room

Dana helped Hannigan to his feet. The movement seemed to give the big journalist a little more energy, and he hitched up his pants and smoothed down his T-shirt.

Dana smiled at him. "Looking good, Baby."

Hannigan gave her a weak smile in return. "You're full o'shit, Dana."

"A speciality of mine."

A large explosion detonated outside and the plate glass doors shook. One of the smaller tables which had been piled onto the barricade was dislodged and fell to the ground with a clatter.

"Jesus," said Hannigan. "Maybe we better get upstairs."

"Yeah," said Dana, "but…" she looked around at the body of Dave Geddes.

"We better move him somewhere first," said Hannigan.

"The bar?" asked Dana.

"OK. Can you take his feet?"

Dana nodded and bent to take Geddes' weight. Hannigan placed his hands under Geddes' armpits and hefted; there was no need for gentleness now, he thought sadly. Together, they lurched towards the bar, Geddes' frame hanging down between them, Hannigan staggering backwards.

They crossed the threshold into the bar area. Hannigan looked over his shoulder. He spotted the longest of the bar's plush sofas. "There," he gasped, indicating the direction with his head. Dana nodded, and between them they shifted the body across to the sofa, finally heaving it into position. Hannigan tried to catch his breath. Dana stepped forward and gently closed Geddes' eyelids. She looked around. "Need a sheet or something to cover him."

Hannigan looked around too. "Can't see anything in here. What about in there?" he gestured towards the small ante room.

"I'll take a look." Dana walked across and disappeared out of the bar and into the adjoining room.

Steve Hannigan looked down at the body of his colleague. "Well man, I guess the luck was always gonna run out sooner or later for one of us. Thanks for everything, buddy." He laid his hand on Geddes' shoulder.

Dana rushed back into the bar, looking flustered and pale.

Hannigan looked up. "What?"

Dana jerked her thumb over her shoulder, back in the direction that she'd just come from. "There are people outside, in the alley. They're trying to get in."

Hannigan dashed across to her and together they went back into the ante room. The locked door was rattling on its hinges and knocking against the metal beer kegs which were braced against it from the inside. "Jesus," Hannigan muttered. A steady beating came from the other side of the door; it sounded to Hannigan like more than one person was hammering at it

Dana shot him a concerned look. "What should we do?"

"What can we do?"

As they looked helplessly at each other, a faint voice suddenly came from the other side. "Can you hear us? Anybody there?"

Dana started forwards. "That's… that's Rachel!"

Hannigan looked across at her, quizzically.

"My colleague." Dana rushed across to the beer kegs and leaned in towards the door.

"Hello?" she shouted. "Rach, is that you?"

"Dana? Dana, it's Rach. We're all out here, we need to get back in. Please!"

"Oh my god. OK, hold on!" She started to tug at the first of the beer kegs.

"Wait!" Hannigan was abrupt. "How do we know there aren't any hostiles with them?"

Dana stopped what she was doing and straightened up.

She shouted back through the door, "Rach, are you OK? Are you under…"

"There's nobody holding us at gunpoint out here, if that's what you're asking, but please, let us in for god's sake! It's not safe out here."

Dana looked at Hannigan. The journalist answered her unasked question. "But we don't know if she's lying or not. You would say that if you were being threatened."

Dana considered for a moment. "But there's no way for us to know. There are no windows here. We'll just have to believe her."

"Or…"

Dana cut him off. "Or they'll fucking die out there," and started to move the beer keg once more. Hannigan stared for a moment and then bent down to help her.

From outside, "Please!"

"We're gettin' the door open now, Rach. Hang on."

Between them, Dana and Hannigan managed to move both of the kegs out of the way. There was a key in the door, and bolts secured it at both the top and bottom. Dana turned the key and then bent to slide the bottom bolt, whilst Hannigan reached up to unfasten the top one. They opened the door and Rachel stumbled in, her face flushed with both exertion and relief. Behind her, the others streamed through, in what felt to Dana like a continuous mass. The last of them pushed in through the door and Hannigan slammed it shut, turning the key and sliding the bolts. The beer kegs were pushed back into position. Hannigan turned around; Dana was holding Rachel, who was sobbing into Dana's shoulder with sheer relief. Behind them, the others were moving into the bar. Hannigan frowned; something didn't seem right to him. He walked through into the bar area and cast his eye around. He didn't see Rob, the pilot. Some of the guests had flopped down onto sofas, others were standing around, clearly in some state of shock. He saw the Englishwoman from the bar earlier – a lifetime ago – looking ashen faced. Her daughter had draped her arm across her mother's shoulder. With a sudden start, he caught a glimpse of Geddes' lifeless form on the sofa where they had just laid him. Nobody seemed to have noticed him; they'll think he's still unconscious and out of it, thought Hannigan. But I need to get them out of here.

"OK, folks, let's go and get to the others. They've moved to the restaurant they're building on the fifth floor." He started to shepherd them out of the bar. Behind him, Dana followed, helping Rachel along. Hannigan stood by the entrance to the bar, watching them go. The guests left the bar, crossed the empty lobby and started to ascend the stairs. Outside, the din of the battle continued. Lights flashed and pulsed and screams and shouts could be heard above the general mayhem. With the last of the returnees starting to mount the stairs, Hannigan turned back to the now-empty bar. He stood for a moment, looking at the body of his friend and colleague. "So long, Buddy," he whispered. Then he turned and followed the others.

The Doors

In the restaurant, it was still dark beyond the windows, but the room was intermittently illuminated by regular flashes which the violence outside was continuing to precipitate. The guests were spread haphazardly around. Some slept – or attempted sleep. Some were propped against the walls and stared balefully across the room. Some guests huddled close together and engaged in muted conversation. Tony Johnson surveyed the room from his perch, leaning against the moribund counter.

To his right Sarah Booth was talking quietly to Colin Brazier as he stared vacantly at the far wall. On the other side of the restaurant, Greta Brazier had her arm draped around the shoulders of her sister-in-law. Tricia Brazier's face was buried in her hands and every now and then her shoulders heaved as she let out another sob. Alongside her, Gaby looked pale but composed. She stared fixedly ahead, her hand resting gently on her mother's knee.

Lee Chung, standing alongside Tony Johnson, shook his head softly. This was a nightmare made real.

The relative peace was suddenly shattered by a huge bang from below them, which almost immediately was accompanied by the unmistakable sound of shattering glass. Heads jerked up all around the restaurant. Johnson sprang up from lounging against the bar and was instantly attentive. "That sounded like the doors! Everybody stay where you are. I'll go and investigate."

Oleksanders stepped forward, "I'll come too."

Johnson hesitated a moment, then nodded. "OK." He waved his index finger generally around the shell of the restaurant. "Everybody else – stay put. Please."

With that, he turned on his heel and together with Oleksanders, slipped out of the restaurant, leaving behind a concerned buzz of discussion.

The stairwell was dark and gloomy, with only the weak glow of the emergency lighting illuminating their descent. As they carefully progressed down the stairs, Johnson became aware of an increase in the volume of the violence leaking in from outside. Not worse, he thought, just louder – the doors must definitely have gone. As they reached the second floor, Oleksanders looked across at him; reading his thoughts, Johnson patted the air with the palm of his hand. *Slowly, quietly.* That was the unspoken message which passed between them.

Creeping now, they rounded the corner of the stairs and passed a small landing. They moved on down to the first floor. Johnson could feel some of the humidity of the night air flowing into the empty expanse of the lobby. It carried with it the whiff of civil unrest – cordite, smoke, sweat. The sound of rioting echoed from one marble wall of the lobby to another and ricocheted up the stairwell.

Johnson took a deep breath. His heart was pounding in his chest and he felt sweat trickling down his inner arms. He hadn't felt like this since Goose Green. He looked across at Oleksanders; the barman seemed calm and collected, his gangly frame not betraying any signs of tension. Johnson was impressed – a good guy to have in the trenches alongside you. It was a well-worn phrase, but felt absolutely appropriate now, as they turned the final corner and prepared themselves for what they might find.

Below them the once-pristine floor of the lobby was littered with thousands of shards of glass. The fragments caught and reflected the light – both the low level emergency lighting and the more uneven light of the flashes from outside. Johnson was reminded of diamonds covering a desert floor. He crouched by the balustrade and alongside him, Oleksanders did the same. Cautiously, they peered around, but even as they did so, Johnson realised that the lobby must be empty – there was no way that anyone could walk across that floor without the tell-tale sound of crunching glass, and of that, there was no sign. Flicking his gaze around the lobby's expanse, he was able to confirm his initial feeling; he felt his tensed muscles relax, just a little. So far so good, but still no room for complacency, he thought.

He turned his attention to the shattered glass doors; there was no indication of what had caused their implosion; he suspected it was as tlikely to have been a blast of sonic energy from a nearby explosion as it was to have been caused by a physical impact. There was certainly no indication that anything had come through the doors. He was somewhat gratified to note that the barricade whose construction he had supervised was still largely intact; some of the top-most pieces of furniture which had been piled up had been blown off the rest of the barricade and now lay, smashed and marooned, on the floor, but most of the structure was still intact. The shards of glass must have been blasted through the various cracks and gaps in the barricade, he reasoned, and that must also mean that quite a bit hadn't made it through. He imagined a great fall of glass debris on the other side of the barrier, piled up like freshly driven snow and thought that it was probably now also acting as a defence for the hotel – trying to get across such a potentially lethal carpet would be foolhardy to say the least. And that was if anybody even tried to; he was beginning to suspect that the opposing forces outside were too tied up in their own war to worry about hotels in their peripheral vision. Maybe somebody might try to get in to use the hotel as a sniping post, or to take refuge, but they had survived this long without anybody from outside infiltrating them. He began to feel the stirrings of hope and then he noticed something which lifted his spirits higher still. Beyond the barricade, past the shattered doors and cutting through the humid air outside, he could see the first faint signs of dawn breaking.

War of Attrition

A clamour surrounded Johnson and Oleksanders as they re-entered the restaurant. Tony Johnson held up his hands and appealed for quiet.

"OK, the situation – as far as we can make out – is that the main doors have been blown in…" There were some gasps, "…but, but… most of the barricade has held up well and we didn't see any signs of any intruders." Gasps were replaced by mutterings of relief. Johnson held his hands up again, "And the dawn is starting to break. It's getting lighter out there. We may find that the authorities have a better chance of re-asserting control in daylight."

"Is that what we want to happen?" somebody shouted. "These guys have unleashed a war on their own doorstep."

Johnson nodded. "There will, of course, be differing views on which side is in the moral right. That isn't for me to say. What I do care about is that some element of control is re-established to make the streets safe again – at least temporarily – and to keep you all safe until we can get you out of here." There were nods and murmurs of assent.

"So what happens now?" called a voice from the crowd.

The Head of Security looked across at Lee Chung, who inclined his head slightly. "We wait," said Johnson, "and we watch."

With that, he moved through the crowd in front of him and across to one of the windows. He turned once again to the other inhabitants of the restaurant. "OK, I know we have asked everybody to keep clear, but I'm going to move up to the window and take a quick look out. It'll help us to gauge what's going on, but can I please ask everyone to stay back from it, just as a safety precaution?" The small crowd in front of him took an instinctive step backwards en masse. Despite the gravity of the situation, Johnson felt a slight smile play around the edge of his mouth; the herd would usually obey somebody in a position of authority, but not usually quite so quickly. He advanced towards the glass, through which, a thin line of milky light was now spreading. Johnson dropped to his knees and, inclining his head, carefully peered out.

Outside, the gathering light was starting to illuminate the scene in the street below. He could see the mass of security forces, occupying the space immediately outside the hotel. Craning his head to the right he could see where the demonstrators had been corralled, but the protestors themselves couldn't be seen; they were hidden behind a huge version of the hotel barricade he had created earlier. There were still some shots being fired, but they seemed fewer in number than previously, and the occasional petrol bomb was thrown from behind the barricade but he could see that this situation was developing into a stand-off. He looked back across to his left, and his gaze played across the mass of security personnel. He reckoned that they outnumbered the protestors at least three to one. Presumably protestors had been dropping away – either slipping away from the protest or dropping away in a more macabre fashion – throughout the night. Johnson could see only one winner emerging from the confrontation. This was now a war of attrition; surely it was only a matter of time now?

Thoughts

The pale, opalescent light coming through the window illuminated constellations of dust motes floating in the air. Colin, with his legs stretched out on the floor in front of him, watched them wordlessly. Sarah sat to his right hand side; he'd appreciated her words of comfort and now he just appreciated her presence. The air in the restaurant was fetid and rank; dusty and carrying the odour of sweat and fear, but he could smell Sarah's perfume, and it comforted him. Over on the other side of the restaurant, he could see Greta sitting alongside Tricia. Their heads were back against the wall, eyes closed, but he doubted they were sleeping. Gaby lay on the floor, her head in her mother's lap. Colin's eyes drifted back to Greta; he supposed he should feel guilty, but he didn't feel any emotion at all towards Greta. He liked her and he wished her well, but now, in this intense atmosphere, he realised that he didn't feel any kind of spark of emotion towards her. But, still, he felt a stab of guilt. Should he move across to be with her? Their marriage, though new, was already rocky. That much was obvious, and the events of this evening seemed to have catalysed its ending. He let out an audible sigh.

"You OK?" asked Sarah, looking across at him, with concern.

"Just thinking."

"Graham?" she asked, her concerned frown deepening.

He nodded. White lie territory, he thought. He felt a second stab of guilt. Of course he should have been thinking about his brother at this point. Isn't that what any – *normal?* – person would have been doing?

"Oh, Colin." Sarah's concern for him was genuine, he could sense that, but whether it was platonic, or something more visceral, he didn't know.

"We were never close," he said, the words tumbling out as he tried to move away from his lie. "Never saw eye to eye. In fact, we had long periods where we didn't speak. Officially."

"But he was still your brother."

"He was." He surprised himself by choking back a sob, a genuine one, at the end of his sentence.

Sarah went to say something but Colin pre-empted her. "I'm OK, I'm OK. Thank you."

He stood up, as much for something to do as to stretch his legs. Across the restaurant, Greta opened her eyes. Briefly, they made eye contact and then both looked away, both embarrassed.

At the Window

Rachel was pale but composed. As she finished telling Dana what had happened outside, she took a sip of the water that she was holding.

"And he just ran off and left you all?" asked Dana, open-mouthed. Rachel nodded. "What a fucking coward," Dana finished.

Rachel looked into her friend's eyes. "Dana, it was hell out there. People aren't really in full control of themselves."

"Bullshit! *You* didn't run off, Rach. *You* didn't leave all these other people to fend for themselves." She swept her arm around the restaurant. "These people owe you their lives, so don't go making excuses for Rob. He let you all down."

Rachel was silent.

"I wonder where he is now?" mused Dana. Rachel shrugged her shoulders.

"Knowing him, he'll survive," Dana said, "Rats always do." She stood up and stretched out her arms and her back, yawning in the process. She wandered over to where Tony Johnson was still cautiously peeking through the window.

He looked up. "Hi Dana, probably best if you stay back, if that's OK?"

Dana stopped, held up her palms apologetically and emphasised her Texan drawl. "Ain't comin' any closer, ah promise." She smiled.

"Thanks," said Johnson, "No point in us both taking a risk."

"How's it looking?" Dana asked, her accent back to normal.

"I think we're reaching the end game," said Johnson, peering through the glass once more. "The army and police have got the demonstrators cornered, and there are far more of them than there are of the protestors. Also, the daylight should swing the odds in the army's favour. Helicopters, snipers – they'll all function better in the light."

"So how do you think it's gonna end?"

"Hard to say – it depends on whether the army is prepared to give the rest of them safe passage, or whether the demonstrators would accept it if they did. If so, it could be over quite soon."

"And if not?"

Johnson made a face. "It could get messy. Very messy."

Dana gave a short bark of a laugh. "Ha! Like it ain't messy enough already?"

Some people from around the restaurant looked up and across at them.

Johnson reddened slightly. "A whole lot messier, then."

Dana nodded. "I knew what you meant," she said quietly. "Let's just hope it doesn't come to that."

"You and me both," said Johnson.

They stood in silence for a moment. Dana popped a stick of chewing gum into her mouth. "Let me know if I can help any," she said, and with a slight wave of her hand, moved away.

Johnson watched her go and then turned to look back out of the window again.

Sisters-in-Law

Later, she thought it must have been some kind of sixth sense which had made her open her eyes when she had done; Greta had been deeply exhausted but even so, she had only drowsed fitfully for the last half an hour or so. The ambient sounds carrying on in the restaurant around her continued to filter into her consciousness. As she awoke from her drowse, she saw her husband, exactly in her eyeline. For a moment, they made eye contact, and then Greta switched her gaze, staring dead ahead, neither moving nor blinking. She reminded herself that the man had just lost his brother but even so, even with that mitigation, she knew that their relationship was over. After all, in any healthy relationship, shouldn't she have been at his side now, caring for her bereaved husband? Maybe so but, she realised, with a twinge of guilt, all she felt right now was relief. The guilt passed after a fleeting moment; the feeling of relief, she noted, remained.

She pulled her attention away from Colin on the other side of the room and looked across at Tricia. Her sister-in-law was apparently sleeping. Greta rolled those words around in her mind. *Sister-in-law*. Was that still the case? The link between them was tenuous now, to say the least, with Tricia's husband dead and her own husband now almost certainly occupying that position in name only. Her link with the two brothers was virtually over, just as she had started to get to know Tricia and Gaby. How strange, she thought, that only a few hours ago she had walked into the hotel with her husband to meet this stranger and now hers and Colin's lives had started to diverge, whilst she felt a strange kinship with – almost a sense of protection towards - Tricia and her daughter.

Tricia slept on, her breathing light, her face a pale and drawn shadow. Her eyelids flickered and her mouth twitched slightly. Her hand made a slight clawing movement at Greta's side, and Greta shifted her position slightly to avoid touching it. Tricia made a slight whimpering noise in her sleep and was then quiet.

Very rarely could one person know what another was dreaming but on this occasion, Greta had absolutely no doubt about what was replaying in Tricia's mind. Greta could have wept for her.

Daylight

There was no doubt now that the dawn had broken. The light filtering in through the window had changed from a milky opalescence to an orange glow, throwing a warming hue onto the faces of the people gathered in the unfinished restaurant. To Sarah, it had the feel of the end of a long-haul flight. That point when the cabin crew moved around the aircraft, prompting passengers to open their window blinds, with the result that some passengers started to stir whilst others remained resolutely asleep. Looking around the shell of the restaurant now, Sarah saw the same types of activity; some stretching and yawning, some rubbing of eyes, some people just flat-out. Beside her, Rachel was now asleep. Sarah hadn't slept, but she wasn't surprised; her body hadn't adjusted yet to the end of her own latest long-haul flight which she had completed only the day before, so she still felt like she was on flight time. Her eyes were scratchy and tired, though. When she was awake all night, she expected to see the suffused blue/green glow of the cockpit instruments, and the sympathetic flight deck lighting. The last few hours had, by contrast, involved, alternately, harsh lighting, darkness, emergency lighting, flashes and, above all, a constant background level of alertness which was never normally the case when flying over the Atlantic or central Asia in the dead of night.

Moving very carefully, so that she didn't disturb Rachel, who continued to doze next to her, she manoeuvred her left arm and rubbed her eyes for some temporary respite. It helped, a little, but they still felt gritty and raw. She turned her head to look where daylight was now starting to filter through into the room and as she did so, there was a sudden flash of light from outside. A fraction of a second later there was a large bang and she felt the building rock. Several things happened simultaneously; she saw Tony Johnson, in position by the window, reel backwards; she heard a collective gasp emanate from amongst the people gathered in the restaurant; and alarms started to shrill. Rachel, next to her, was instantly awake, jerking her head up, off her chest.

"What... what happened?"

"I don't know," said Sarah grimly, as she slowly got to her feet, "but it didn't sound good."

Alarms continued to sound, reverberating between the walls and the ceiling. Around the restaurant, others were also now standing, faces almost universally concerned and worried. In front of her, Tony Johnson slowly rolled from the crouched position he'd assumed after flinging himself away from the window and tentatively sat up. He looked dazed, like a punch-drunk boxer. Sarah saw Dana scuttling across to his aid. From around the room came a chorus of concern: "What's happened?", "What the hell was that?", "Oh my god."

The building had stopped shaking but, from down below, there came a loud crash and several popping sounds. Sarah moved across to Johnson and Dana. The security man seemed to have recovered his senses; Dana stood anxiously by his side.

"Thoughts?" asked Sarah. Pilot training taught one to be economical with words, to focus on the key issues. Johnson looked strained. "Bomb," he said simply, "or mortar. Some sort of explosive projectile."

Sarah and Dana exchanged concerned glances. Tony Johnson read their thoughts. "Yes," he said, "There could be a fire."

<u>Downstairs</u>

Once more, Tony Johnson found himself descending the stairs with Oleksanders; unlike the previous occasion though, this time they were running down them. He felt his bad ankle protesting as he leaped down two steps at a time; alongside him, Oleksanders, with his longer stride length, was often taking them three at a time. But Johnson knew before he reached the ground floor what they would find. He could smell it. He could hear it. He could feel it. Fire.

As he moved down he could hear the crackle of burning wood, and the smell of it was redolent in his nostrils. They rounded the final corner of the stairs, and Johnson's worst fears were confirmed. As the smoke alarms continued to shrill, he surveyed the scene before him; the makeshift barricade was ablaze, orange flame licking across the polished mahogany, oak and pine surfaces. The wood crackled and fizzed as it burned, tens of thousands' of dollars' worth of high grade furniture turning to black smoke and ash. Twenty-four hours previously, that would have been a huge issue for Johnson, but now the financial implications were the least of his concerns. Oleksanders stopped alongside him. He made a one word assessment. "Shit."

Johnson quickly scanned the lobby. The ice diamonds of glass from the shattered doors still covered the floor, but now the various elements of the barricade were also strewn across it. Most of the pieces were ablaze. Portions of the ceiling were hanging down, drooping dangerously under their own weight. Portraits and fittings had been blasted off the walls. Plaster littered the floor. The reception desk had been blown to pieces. Johnson shook his head slowly. This must have been one hell of a blast, he thought. He looked across at the shattered glass doors. The remnants of the barricade remained in front of them, but it was on fire; beyond, he could just about make out the street. He caught glimpses of figures, mostly in black riot gear. He registered the occasional sound of a shot, but it was hard to hear above the combined din of the hotel's smoke alarm sirens and the crackle of the burgeoning fires, and he could barely see through the heat haze and the black smoke swirling from the burning furniture.

His eyes tracked back into the lobby, moving automatically to the walls, where he knew the fire extinguishers were located, but he realised that it was too late; the fires had set in across the lobby and were already beyond the control of amateur firefighters. His thoughts turned instead to escape. He looked back across at Oleksanders. "Whatever's happened to cause this," he nodded towards the lobby where flames where now starting to lick up the walls, "nobody's getting out that way."

Oleksanders spread his hands wide. "So…?"

"So we head back up," said Johnson in a firm tone. "Re-group and re-plan from there." The security man took one last look at the blazing lobby and then, motioning Oleksanders to follow him, set off back up the stairs.

The Realisation

They burst back into the fifth floor restaurant. Nobody now was asleep, nobody was slouching against the walls. Even as Johnson rushed through the door, he could sense the anticipation in the room; there was a movement of bodies towards both him and Oleksanders. Lee Chung scuttled to the front of the surge and, despite his small stature, headed the small crowd to reach Johnson first.

"Tony, Oleksanders – what's happening?"

Johnson answered immediately. "It's bad, Boss."

Lee Chung winced. "OK." His expression was that of a man prepared for the worst.

Johnson looked around hesitantly. A sea of concerned eyes stared back at him. The last thing he wanted to do here was cause a panic, but he had to be truthful; there was no point in sugar coating the reality of what they confronted. He took a deep breath. Lee Chung cracked his knuckles nervously.

"OK… we have taken a hit, I'm not sure what from." There was a murmur of discontent from the people in front of and around him; Lee Chung looked pained. Johnson held up his hands. "I'm sorry to say that a fire has broken out downstairs; the lobby is on fire."

The assembled people broke out into a paroxysm of angst and consternation. There were shouts and even some screams. Johnson held up his hands again and called for calm. "Please… can I ask… please… hello… please…" He wasn't making much progress, so decided more drastic measures were called for.

"Silence!" he bellowed, using every bit of his six foot four inch frame to emphasise the word.

The room before him quietened immediately. Alarms continued to shrill. "Thank you," he said. "Now, listen. The situation is serious but there is no need for us to panic. This is a large hotel and we have time to decide what we need to do. But there is no denying that we face a serious situation. A *critical* situation. We need to think about evacuating, but we won't be able to do so by getting out through the ground floor – the fire is too intense for that. As I say, we do have time to think about what we do, but we need to work quickly. The fire will spread. We *will* have to move. Now, please, I need to talk to Mr Chung to discuss what we do next."

As he finished his address, murmuring started up again across the room. Lee Chung laid a hand on Tony Johnson's arm. "Well done," he said.

Johnson nodded. "Thanks. But now what?"

"The route downstairs is definitely blocked?"

"Definitely. Maybe if we'd all been in the lobby when it happened, we could have got out before the fire started to spread. But then, again, if we'd all been in the lobby…"

He didn't need to finish the sentence; Lee Chung nodded slowly. "Anyway," Johnson continued, "the fire has really taken hold of the downstairs. Maybe one or two people might be able to get through to the rear door, but there's no chance that everyone would get out alive."

"Will it spread?" Chung asked him.

"It will," the security man assented. They both looked at each other, thinking the same thought. An image of Rob Mitchell sprang into Johnson's mind. Mitchell was looking up at him, standing his ground, querulously demanding to see an emergency plan for the tower. Johnson felt a nauseous lurch in the pit of his stomach.

"And the tower's fire escape isn't in place yet," added Johnson in a voice which seemed too quiet for him.

Chung nodded grimly. "So..." he said, "only one thing for it. We have to go up."

<u>Going Up</u>

Dana was slightly breathless as she reached the fifteenth floor. Ten flights of stairs were in part to blame but she liked to think that she was in reasonably good shape and that the curling, acrid smoke rising up from below was the main reason for her gasps. Reluctantly though, she noted that Sarah Booth, ahead of her, seemed to have coped much better with the ascent – like the triathlete that she was. Dana paused to catch her breath and looked back down. A thin line of guests was strung out on the stairwell, slowly making their way up to the fifteenth floor. Way below, she caught a glimpse of Steve Hannigan, the bulky newsman's upturned face gazing up forlornly as he realised how far there still was to go.

Lee Chung beckoned her. "This way please, Dana." She flashed him a smile and moved past him and through the open door, through which daylight was streaming. Daylight. She blinked as she emerged out onto the terrace. Without her sunglasses, she felt dazzled by the bright sunshine, especially having spent so long in the dim glow of emergency lighting and the largely dark restaurant. She shielded her eyes and followed Sarah further out onto the flat expanse before them. Behind her, the hotel's main tower, shrouded by its scaffolding, soared up towards the brilliant blue sky; more guests were now following her out onto the terrace.

In front of her, guests were milling on what was destined to become the rooftop running track. From the streets far below them came the now familiar pops and bangs of the continuing battle, although they were far fewer in number than they had been during the night. Johnson was right, she thought, it felt like the siege was drawing to a close. She shook her head bitterly. Tough shit then, that we're stuck in a burning building just as it all ends.

Thick black smoke was now belching from out of the sides of the hotel below them and rising up on either side of them. She saw Rachel standing in the centre of the terrace and started to walk over towards her, but she stopped in her tracks as she heard a familiar sound. Both women looked up simultaneously, as did many of the others on the rooftop. From the direction of the city centre, a helicopter was clattering its way towards them. Some of the people on the roof started to wave their arms above their heads, but it seemed that the helicopter already had designs on them; it was heading straight towards the hotel. Dana had a fleeting thought about all the violence that had been unleashed over the last twenty-four hours. She didn't doubt that this government had helicopter gunships in its arsenal and, for a moment, she wondered about whether to dart back into the hotel. But then she thought about the pungent smoke rolling up the stairwells; even now people were staggering out onto the terrace, many of them coughing and spluttering. No, she thought, better to stay out here and take our chance. Surely it would be obvious that they were civilians?

The helicopter circled the hotel, keeping a reasonable distance. Dana caught glimpses of it moving around them as it moved in and out of patches of smoke. After a couple of circuits, the black craft moved in closer. Checking us out, Dana thought. She felt reassured by that; if it had sinister intentions, surely it would already have fired on them by now?

She walked across to Rachel. Around her, some people were still manically waving their arms; despite the gravity of the situation, Dana chuckled to herself. It's seen us now, you assholes! she thought. She joined Rachel. Together they watched as the helicopter settled into a low hover some one hundred feet or so above the terrace. Dana felt her hair streaming behind her in the downdraft from the aircraft's rotor blades. Red and green navigation lights flashed rapidly on the helicopter and then flashed again. The craft descended slightly. Dana felt the increased strength of the downdraft on her face; the noise from just above was intense. The navigation lights flashed into action once more. All around her, people were staring up at the chopper, tension writ large on their faces.

Dana saw Sarah Booth dash across to Tony Johnson and shout into his ear. Johnson nodded, then cupped his hands to his mouth and shouted at the top of his voice, "It wants to land. It's going to land!" He started to wave people back from where they stood and the guests dutifully moved back, forming a loosely widening circle. Some of the people looked nervously over their shoulders as they backed towards the hotel, where smoke was now billowing furiously from the tower. The helicopter began its descent, lazily turning as it dropped, eventually settling gently onto its skids in the middle of the flat expanse. The rotors continued to turn at a furious pace.

Dana appraised the craft; it was undoubtedly a police or military helicopter, but painted entirely black and with no distinguishing marks that she could see, it was impossible to tell to which security branch it belonged. It was relatively small, seating four or six people, she guessed. The door on the right hand side of the aircraft opened and a helmeted figure wearing a flight suit jumped out, and ducking their head to avoid the spinning blades, dashed over towards the small knot of people immediately in front of the helicopter. Dana saw Tony Johnson and Lee Chung both rush across towards the figure. Within seconds they were alongside the crew member and engaging in animated discussion. She saw Tony Johnson indicating the people on the rooftop in an expansive gesture. The crew member nodded and pointed back towards the helicopter. Lee Chung stepped away from both Johnson and the airman and scanned the people on the rooftop. Dana saw his eyes alight on somebody and then beckon to them. She followed his line of sight. Tricia Brazier was making a gesture towards herself which Dana immediately recognised as meaning, "Who, me?" Gaby stood alongside her. She looked very pale and to Dana, seemed to be a tiny scrap of a person. Lee Chung nodded vigorously and waved them forward. Tricia moved forward, pushing her daughter ahead of her. Some of the crowd parted to let them through; they seemed to instinctively know what was happening – prioritise the evacuation of children. The airman ushered Tricia and Gaby to the waiting chopper, opened the door immediately behind the pilot and bundled them in. He then climbed in himself. Almost immediately, Dana heard the pitch of the rotors change, the blades flexed upwards and the black craft lifted off. Dana caught a brief glimpse of Gaby's forlorn face staring from the window before the helicopter dipped its nose and still rising, moved off, back in the direction it had come from, towards the city centre. As it went it scattered some of the surging black smoke coming from the hotel. Within seconds it was a fading black dot, although the noise of its passing lingered, as it echoed from wall to wall over the densely packed city.

Tony Johnson walked across to the centre of the terrace, to the spot from where the chopper had just departed. He beckoned to the frightened guests to draw in towards him and prepared to address them.

The Terrace

If the noise from the small utility helicopter which had evacuated Tricia and Gaby was intense, then the noise from the Chinooks was absolutely deafening. Sound washed across the rooftop terrace as the three huge transports flew in from the east. Johnson had already marshalled the guests into three separate lines as close to the hotel tower as the billowing smoke would permit, leaving the central area clear for the Chinooks to land. He'd faced some resistance; understandably, many people had been reluctant to venture too close to the tower, from which oily, black smoke was now relentlessly surging. But needs must; with the help of the flight attendants – this after all, was their natural metier – he'd been firmly insistent and the people had been expertly shepherded back towards the wall.

Above and off to one side of the terrace, the three helicopters slowed in their approach, flaring their noses as they did so. Two of them adopted a hover, their twin rotors effortlessly keeping the massive machines aloft. The third Chinook had not flared its nose to the same degree as its companions and continued its trajectory, bringing it in towards the hotel's roof. The noise now was absolutely incredible.

As it came in for its landing, Johnson could see the two pilots behind the windshield; they were wearing khaki flight helmets, dark visors pulled down over their eyes. Johnson watched as they expertly brought the giant helicopter in for its touchdown. Suddenly, and unexpectedly, he was back in the Falklands and watching, helpless and appalled, as the Sea King and Wessex helicopters squeezed into unimaginably tight landings to evacuate casualties from the battlefield. Now, back in the present, he heard the same clatter of rotors and saw the tight, concentrated expression on the pilots' faces that he'd seen then. He had to almost physically detach his consciousness away from that long-ago day in 1982 and pull it back to the present; the Chinook settled onto its wheels in the middle of the terrace, rotors swirling and dust flying up from the rooftop. Meanwhile thick, acrid smoke continued to pour from the hotel tower. The Chinook's rear ramp lowered, and Johnson waved the first line of guests forward. There were just over forty of them in this first group. In his shouted discussions with the airman from the utility helicopter, he'd been told that the Chinooks were on the way and that each one could carry up to 55 people out. A crewman ran down the ramp and started to urge the evacuees forward; they did not need a lot of persuading. Johnson watched as the guests ran and jogged into the belly of the helicopter. The guests had been randomly allocated into the three lines, and he saw Greta Brazier amongst those rushing up the ramp. Colin Brazier though, had hung back and joined the third line, which contained all of the airline flight crew, who to their credit, had insisted to him that they stayed behind to help supervise the airlift.

The last of the guests headed up the ramp, the crewman spoke into his helmet microphone, gave Johnson a thumbs up and then jumped onto the ramp himself. The Chinook began to lift off the ground even before the ramp had started to close. Johnson felt the vibrations of the helicopter's signature *wokka-wokka* sound bouncing around his skull as it gained first height and then speed and started to fly off to the east. No sooner had it left the vicinity of the hotel than the second Chinook, which had been hovering on station alongside the third transport, floated in to make its own landing.

The process was swiftly repeated, the guests in the second line streaming aboard the helicopter as its ramp was lowered. Johnson was gratified to note that there hadn't been any panic; nobody had tried to claw their way to the front of the queue and he was proud of the guests' orderly behaviour. He looked around him; he had a nagging feeling that something wasn't right, but he couldn't put his finger on what it was. Oleksanders went past him in the line boarding the transport. Their eyes briefly met and Johnson nodded and raised his hand. Oleksanders grinned and gave him a thumbs up as he shuffled forward. As the last of the evacuees boarded, the crewman gave the thumbs up, the ramp started to raise and the

Chinook powered into the air, the throbs of its rotors pounding around the terrace. Johnson watched it go, still unable to shake off his feeling of unease.

Now the third and final helicopter moved in for its pick-up. It settled into place and deployed its ramp. Johnson was relieved; the smoke was now coming out of the tower thick and fast. He wouldn't want to be in the hotel for much longer; the fire seemed to be spreading very quickly now. Johnson waved the final line of evacuees forward and watched them as they moved into the interior of the Chinook. The airline flight crew brought up the rear, shepherding the other guests up the ramp. He watched as Sarah, Dana, Rachel, Ryan and the others went past. They'd done a great job he thought, in helping to keep the other guests calm and collected.

Dana followed the others into the spacious but functional interior of the Chinook. Two rows of red webbing-based seats lined each wall of the interior of the aircraft's fuselage. The evacuated people were already beginning to gingerly sit themselves in position, largely at the insistent urging of the crew member who had waved them aboard. In his khaki flight suit and helmet, Dana thought he looked otherworldly. He continued, with great assertiveness, to point to vacant seats which were quickly filled up. Dana found a lap belt and fastened it around her midriff. As she did so, she chuckled to herself. This guy would have a great future at the airline, she thought – he was getting people into their seats and belted up far faster than she and her colleagues had ever managed. She tried to catch Rachel's eye to see if she had also noticed his efficacy, but she wasn't looking in Dana's direction. No matter, she could catch up with her later, she thought.

Dana sank back into the yielding red canvas of the seat. She finally felt like she was able to start to relax. In a few seconds the helicopter would be airborne and sweeping them away from the hotel, away from the chaos in the streets outside. Where they were heading she had no idea, but she knew it would be a damn sight safer than where they were leaving.

The ramp started to close and, as it did so, she felt a slight lurch in the pit of her stomach as the Chinook began to shift its weight from its wheels to its rotors. She caught a glimpse of blue sky disappearing outside as the ramp finished closing. Dim strip lighting cast the interior of the transport in a pallid yellow glow; it smelt of oil and stale sweat, but that was of no consequence to Dana. She closed her eyes and exhaled deeply as she felt the helicopter lift off the roof. She could almost feel the cares and responsibilities of the past twelve hours washing away from her shoulders. The noise inside the Chinook was thunderous; there was no prospect of being able to speak to anybody so when she opened her eyes again she contented herself with looking around the cabin and savouring the moment of escape. She looked across at where Sarah was sitting and wondered whether the pilot would be relishing this unexpected trip in a new type of aircraft. A little further along, Rachel sat with Ryan and Nigel. Dana was proud to be a part of this crew; at least the part of the crew that didn't include Rob Mitchell. She still couldn't believe that he'd abandoned his charges during their abortive escape bid, with a man being killed in the process. Surely such a gross dereliction of leadership would mean the end of his career? She hoped so; he deserved it.

Dana contrasted Rob's behaviour with that of Tony Johnson; there was no comparison. The big security man had proved to be everything that Rob Mitchell wasn't – solid, dependable, resourceful, generous of spirit. She looked around the cabin to seek him out. She didn't see him sitting in the row of seats opposite her. She leaned out of her seat a little and looked to her left. No sign. She looked to the right. He wasn't there, either. She felt her heart quicken; he must be on board, surely. She hurriedly re-scanned the seats opposite and then double checked to either side. There could be no doubt; Tony Johnson was not on board the Chinook.

She unstrapped her lap belt and stood up. The helicopter's floor was vibrating and shaking, and she paused for a moment to get her balance, but over a decade's worth of practice walking down airliner aisles during turbulence sometimes came in handy. The people who had been sitting on either side of her looked up questioningly but she ignored them and started off towards the rear of the cabin. The air loadmaster who had shepherded them on board must have caught her movement out of the corner of his eye and abruptly turned his head towards Dana. He gestured angrily to her to return to her seat. Dana set her face and continued towards him. Another role reversal, she thought. He started to rise out of his seat, to intercept her and Dana carried steadfastly on, ready to bellow into his ear that they had left somebody behind.

Goose Green

Tony Johnson had watched the airline flight crew board the helicopter with a sense of grim satisfaction, of a job well done. He was preparing to follow them when the sub-conscious concern that had been eating away at him since they had been on the terrace suddenly exploded into full sentience; he had watched every single person board each of the three Chinooks and now he suddenly realised that there was one person who had not filed past.

Steve Hannigan. A big, black, bear of a man, the newsman was unmistakable, and, suddenly, so was his absence. The air loadmaster was already on board the Chinook, and the ramp was starting to close. Johnson had a split second to make his decision.

Suddenly, it was almost forty years ago again, and the battle was nearing its climax. The paras in A Company were still pinned down on the lower slopes of Darwin Hill when the order came to advance towards the little settlement of Goose Green. Around him, his fellow soldiers started to carefully move forward. Johnson did likewise and emerged from his cover, a straggly gorse bush, but, after hours of immobility and inactivity, his muscles had seized up. His legs just wouldn't work, and he felt his ankle give with a sickening lurch. Suddenly, he was face down in the mud, with a searing pain in his ankle and his vision clouding over. He tried to crawl back to his cover, but he had lost all sense of direction and the pain was debilitating. He lay there, with the earthy tang of soil in his mouth and the sound of unseen bullets streaking past, uncomfortably close. Somewhere in his mind, he knew that he was done for. He closed his eyes and waited for the inevitable. Suddenly he was seized by what felt like a great, irresistible force, but the noise in his ear wasn't that of a bullet nor of his own blood, but an English voice screaming, "On your feet, soldier!" The next thing he knew, he was being hauled to his feet – indescribable pain again – and dragged back to cover. He became dimly aware of a medic attending to him. The last image he registered before the morphine kicked in and his eyes closed was of the para who had plucked him from the mud moving off, back to join the fray.

Now, as he watched the ramp close, the image of the para returning to the battle flashed back to him for a split second. He knew he should have died that day, but somebody hadn't given up on him, hadn't left him to fate's course, had given him another chance. The ramp was still closing as Johnson turned away from the giant helicopter and dashed back towards the blazing tower.

<u>Mission</u>

Johnson was already diving into the midst of the choking black smoke emanating from the hotel's giant main tower when he heard the unmistakable sound from behind him of the Chinook's rotors changing in pitch as they lifted the beast into the air. Ahead of him the smoke churned and twisted as it was simultaneously pulled in two different directions – one straight up the tower, where it swirled onwards and upwards, and the other out of the door onto the rooftop terrace, where it also escaped upwards, but into the sapphire sky. The smoke was acrid and pungent and stung Johnson's eyes. He wiped them with the back of his hand, took a lungful of relatively clear air and then, gripping the handrail of the staircase tightly, started to make his way down the stairwell.

The smoke thickened as he went, wrapping itself around him in its deadly, sooty, cloak. His eyes smarted even more, and he felt tears welling up in both eyes. He had to take a breath, but almost didn't dare to. He threw his right arm across his mouth and nose and breathed out into the crook of his arm; then he breathed in, sucking in air through the corners of his mouth. He coughed and retched. The smoke was far, far worse than it had been during their ascent up the stairs several minutes earlier. The fire had clearly taken a deep hold on the hotel, but he was relieved to see that there was no evidence of flames immediately around him; it seemed that it was the lower floors which were on fire, and the blaze had not yet spread this high. Still, the smoke alone was almost overpowering. He moved on, pressing down the stairs as fast as he dared. Visibility was bad now, and getting worse. He could make out the individual stairs, but only just. Particles of ash settled on his lips, and he hurriedly brushed them away with distaste; there was no telling where that ash had come from.

He realised he had lost track of how far he had descended. When he'd set out, he'd reminded himself to keep track of each 90 degree turn that he made on the stairwell, but the smoke had taken up all of his attention, and he realised he didn't know which floor he was on. It was a mistake; he just hoped it wouldn't prove fatal. He paused for a moment, unsure whether to continue, but then he heard that voice from Goose Green – "On your feet, soldier!" – and took another gasp of oily air and pressed on. He was sweating very heavily and he could feel his heart beating at what felt like an unhealthily frenetic rate. His muscles ached and screamed and he felt the claustrophobic confines of an underwater swimmer who'd stayed down too long and was desperate to break the surface. He could barely see now, and was only progressing by feeling his way down the stairwell, both with his hands on the rail and his feet on the steps. His foot reached the broad expanse of one of the 90 degree landings. He started to tentatively move to his left to tackle the next flight of stairs when his right foot made contact with something. The something was big and yielding. He knelt down and groped on the floor in front of him. A leg. He groped some more. An arm. He moved his hands up the arm and found a shoulder. Moving up still further, he reached a neck. He felt for a pulse. It was there. Faint, but it was there. The smoke cleared a little and he caught a glimpse of Steve Hannigan's face. His eyes were closed and he could almost have looked peaceful, were it not for the rivulet of clotted blood which had streamed down one side of his face; evidently a wound from where he had fallen. The guy must have succumbed to his exhaustion or the smoke and collapsed on the stairs, thought Johnson. Relief at finding his target flooded through Johnson's body, but only temporarily. He thought about the route back, and he thought about Hannigan's bulk, but he knew he had no option. "On your feet, soldier!" he snarled, as much to himself as to Hannigan. Carrying the newsman was out of the question, so he felt for bot armpits, hooked his forearms underneath and, staggering backwards, began to drag the American back up the stairs.

A Sense of Direction

From her seat, Sarah could see Dana remonstrating with the crewman. She was making a lot of hand gestures and clearly shouting into his ear, trying to make herself heard both through the thickness of the crewman's helmet and the din of the Chinook's rotors and engines. Sarah saw her colleague repeatedly pointing towards the rear of the helicopter. Several times, Sarah looked in the direction in which she was pointing, but all she saw was the helicopter's raised ramp. Alongside her, Rachel patted her arm and gave her a quizzical look. Sarah shrugged to her in response. She had absolutely no idea what was going on, but what she did know was that Dana was definitely in one of her feisty moods. When she was like this, Sarah knew she wouldn't take no for an answer. The serious body language from Dana continued, until she finally saw the crewman nod. Sarah watched as the crewman swung the boom microphone beneath his helmet into position and spoke into it, then motioned Dana back to her seat. This time Dana obliged, and carefully picked her way across the helicopter's vibrating floor to retake her seat.

Dana had only just finished strapping herself in when Sarah felt the Chinook lurch and she experienced the familiar sensation of an aircraft banking around a tight circle. She felt her jaw start to sag as they pulled through the turn, a few g-forces momentarily building up as they did so. This was a much tighter turn than they ever managed in the Airbus, and she was reminded of her days in the University Air Squadron, when she would fling the aerobatic little Bulldog trainers around the leaden grey Yorkshire skies. Her pilot's sense of direction told her that they were now heading back exactly on the reverse of the course they had just taken. She realised that they were going back to the hotel. Leaning across to Rachel, she shouted into her ear to let her know what she had surmised. She looked surprised but nodded. Sarah noticed that Rachel was continually clasping and re-clasping her hands together.

Heat

Tony Johnson had never been so tired in his life, nor so hot. He felt like he was wreathed in his own sweat; it cascaded down his forehead and into his eyes. His hair was soaking wet and he could feel great rivers of sweat pouring down his back. His arms and back ached horribly from pulling his burden up the stairs. All the time, the smoke from below continued to rush up the central stairwell, great clouds of writhing, asphyxiating black doom which spread like a thick blanket across each landing that it encountered in its path. His throat was raw from coughing and his breath came in gasps now. His eyes streamed and he felt a weakness in his legs - the first stirrings of a blood sugar low. But he carried on lurching from step to step, dragging the unconscious bulk of Steve Hannigan after him. Hannigan bumped up the stairs, his head slumped into his chest. Despite his tribulations, Johnson paused occasionally to check that there was a rise and fall in that chest; each time he was rewarded by faint movement. *Surely it couldn't be much further now?* He bitterly regretted not having been able to keep track of the number of floors he had moved down.

He rounded another corner and suddenly his spirits soared; at the top of the next flight of stairs the smoke was escaping through an open doorway; he was almost back at the rooftop terrace. The knowledge spurred him on and he felt an extra burst of energy and a kick of adrenaline.

"Come on, come on!" he muttered to himself, "Almost there, come… on!" With a final heave, he managed to get Hannigan up the last step and onto the flat of the landing. Christ, the guy was going to be absolutely black and blue with bruises after this, he thought as he finally dragged the American through the doorway and onto the blessed relief of the terrace. He laid down his charge as gently but quickly as he could, and then doubled up, hands on his knees and coughed and coughed for what seemed like an eternity. Smoke continued to billow through the doorway and wash over them, so he grabbed hold of Hannigan one final time and pulled him into the centre of the terrace. Behind him, the smoke continued to soar and surge out of the tower, blackening almost the whole of the sky; only occasional glimpses of blue sky beyond the nightmarish scene could now be seen.

He slumped onto his knees and coughed some more. His head ached as badly as his back and arms. His decision to go back for Hannigan had been an instantaneous, instinctive one; he hadn't given any thought as to what would happen if he was successful in getting him back to the relative safety of the terrace. The Chinook was long gone and there was no other escape route. The sickening thought started to occur to him that, by rescuing Hannigan, all he had done was to postpone the inevitable. They would just have longer to wait before death embraced them. He buried his head in his hands and shed tears of frustration.

Hope

He still had his head in his hands when he first heard it; the clattering noise in the distance, faint but unmistakable. The sound of a Chinook. He lifted his head and rose from his squatting position to his full height. Beside him Steve Hannigan lay, battered and bruised but alive. Johnson turned through a slow 360 degrees, trying to scan the skies, but frustrated by the drifting smoke. He cursed and decided to listen instead. Standing motionless, he could hear the deep crackle of the building burning behind and beneath him. Beyond that, the noise of the diminishing skirmishes in the streets around the hotel drifted up; he could tell that the violence was now almost played out. The security forces would be conducting a mopping up operation and damping down the last of the resistance. Several hours ago that would have taken up all of his attention, but now it barely registered. He tried to screen out the din from below and to his sides and concentrate instead solely on the noise from the transport helicopter. He strained to hear; was it coming closer? It was hard to tell; the sound washed around and between the skyscrapers, bouncing off walls and other structures, so that it sounded like the Chinook was travelling in many different directions at once. After several seconds of attentive listening, he concluded that the sounds were getting louder – the helicopter, he became sure, was heading his way.

He felt helpless. With the swirling smoke causing such poor visibility, there was no prospect of him being able to directly signal to the chopper, to try to attract its attention. Instead he had to hope that his or Hannigan's presence had been missed, and the Chinook was returning to collect them. All he could do was to wait. He squatted down beside Hannigan. "Hang on in there, mate. I think they're coming for us." He patted the newsman on the arm as he lay there, helpless on the rooftop. He didn't know if Hannigan could hear him but it felt good to be able to offer some reassurance. He knew that it was as much for his own benefit as for the prone American's. But within seconds, there was no doubt that the Chinook was coming for them; the noise was becoming overwhelming but he still couldn't see the huge helicopter, the smoke was too thick for that. He started to feel relief course through him, but no sooner had that emotion started to take hold than he was seized with a sudden fear. How was it going to land? He looked around him; the smoke, although drifting in places, was extremely thick. How on earth could anybody – even the most skilled pilot – bring a giant aircraft in for a pinpoint landing in conditions like these? And would they risk doing it? Even if the Chinook were empty apart from its crew, there would be at least three people on board, and if it was one of the ones which had previously taken the evacuees away, there would be more like sixty people aboard it. Landing in these conditions to pick up two half-dead foreigners would be a hell of a risk to take. Despite the heat emanating from the hotel's blazing tower, he felt a cold shiver run through him.

The noise from overhead was now absolutely deafening, but its pitch had changed. Johnson realised that he was no longer hearing any kind of Doppler Shift; the Chinook must be hovering overhead. The downdraft from the two sets of rotors was causing the smoke to disperse somewhat, away from the centre of the terrace, but Johnson still couldn't see the helicopter. He stood and strained his eyes, trying to will himself to be able to see through the clouds of smoke, but it was to no avail.

Then, as he stood there, he caught a glimpse of movement from the corner of his eye. He looked in the direction it had come from, but smoke had drifted back over, and he couldn't see anything. He was just starting to doubt himself when almost unbelievably, a voice came from within the smoke. "Hello? Hello?"

After a fraction of a second of sheer disbelief Johnson regained his senses. "Over here! Here! There are two of us!"

A figure emerged from out of the clouds of smoke, a figure wearing a khaki flight suit and helmet. He trailed a length of cable which was attached to a harness around his waist. The crewman from the Chinook, Johnson realised. He strode confidently towards the two stricken men. Johnson knew what to do; despite the intervening years his army training kicked in straight away. Incredible how it was almost hard-wired into him, he thought, even as he was delivering his situation report to the crewman. "Two of us," he stated in clipped tones, holding up two fingers in case the crewman didn't speak any English beyond "Hello". He gestured between himself and Hannigan; the crewman responded with a nod. "Badly injured," said Johnson, pointing at Hannigan. The crewman nodded once more and then spoke into the boom microphone attached to his helmet. He motioned to Johnson to help him with Hannigan. Together, they managed to get the unconscious newsman onto his feet, Johnson holding him upright whilst the crewman produced a harness loop, which he slipped under the big man's armpits. He clipped the other end of the loop to his own harness and then spoke into the microphone again. The crewman wrapped his arms around Hannigan, taking his weight. Johnson stepped away. With a sudden jerk, the crewman and Hannigan were lifted off their feet and started to ascend, up through the patchy smoke. Tony Johnson watched them turn a lazy circle as they went. Very quickly, they were lost from his sight as smoke swirled back across the area they had just moved through.

Johnson was alone now. The noise from the Chinook was deafening, but the biggest sensory impression was the heat that was now pouring out of the hotel tower. A shimmering haze pervaded the rooftop terrace, lending an air of unreality to the scene. Johnson waited patiently but kept glancing nervously across at the tower. The heat coming from it really was extremely intense now. He tried to imagine what was going on above him. Surely the crewman and Hannigan would have reached the Chinook by now? People would be pulling them inside, helping Hannigan. It wouldn't take very long for the crewman to start descending again to collect him, he was sure of that. But it seemed to take an eternity; eventually a pair of boots appeared through the base of the cloud of smoke and the crewman thumped down onto the rooftop, alongside him. Johnson moved across towards him. As he did so, a huge explosion ripped out of the hotel tower, showering them both in fragments of glass and building rubble. Johnson was blown off his feet and onto his back. He was temporarily deafened by the violence of the explosion, so he didn't hear the Chinook's rotors screaming as the pilot fought for control, trying to mitigate the effect of the shockwave which had just rolled across the helicopter. Johnson was dazed and disoriented. Still on his back, he put a hand to his face; it was dripping blood. He didn't know what had just happened, but he was sure he was meant to be with somebody. He tried to sit up but he couldn't move. He lay back and pain washed over him, enveloping the whole of his body in agony. He stared straight up; momentarily the clouds of smoke drifted apart, and for a brief moment he saw the crewman swinging around crazily on his line from the Chinook as the helicopter, regaining stability, started to power away from the hotel, winching up its crewmember as it went. The smoke washed over again as Tony Johnson's eyes slowly closed.

In the Truck

The sound of another Chinook. Two had gone past only minutes apart, now a third was also passing overhead. Instinctively Rob Mitchell looked up, but then realised it was a useless activity; all he saw was the roof of the army transport truck. His nose itched and he brought his handcuffed hands up together so that he could use the thumb of his right hand to alleviate the itch. He looked around the truck once more; it was packed with similarly handcuffed people, all of whom were in a state of disarray and many of whom were carrying injuries. Soft moans emanated from several of them and there was an abundance of blood soaking through tattered clothes, and dripping onto the floor of the truck.

He badly needed to urinate, but he knew that would have to wait, however uncomfortable it made him; pissing over the interior of an army truck could surely only worsen his situation. He wondered where they were being taken. As far as he could understand, he'd been arrested for breaking the curfew. Surely only a minor transgression? He knew though, that the bigger worry would be trying to convince the authorities that he was an innocent bystander and not one of the aggressors, and he suspected that they wouldn't be in much of a mood to listen. The country had virtually been a totalitarian state as it was, before all of this had kicked off, and now they had come dangerously close to losing control of their capital city. They wouldn't be prepared to forgive in a hurry. They would be looking to make examples of those they had caught. *Pour encourager les autres*, he thought with a shiver.

The truck rumbled along, bouncing over potholes, with the occasional swerve, no doubt to avoid debris in the road from the previous night. He found himself wondering whether the rioting had spread to the outlying areas beyond the city, and if so, whether they were now back under control as the city appeared to be. He had no way of knowing, but he was pleased to have something to think about; if nothing else, it took his mind off the ache in his bladder.

Landing

Colin breathed a sigh of relief as he felt the Chinook touch down. The ramp had started to lower almost at the moment of landing. Beyond the ramp he could see emergency vehicles, an ambulance at their head. Two medical personnel charged up the ramp and attended immediately to the injured crewman. His face was badly lacerated and he seemed to have sustained injuries as he was swept through the skies as the helicopter made its escape from the blazing hotel. The crewman was swiftly evacuated and then Steve Hannigan, who had lain unconscious on the floor of the Chinook for the duration of its short flight, was next to be taken out.

All of the other passengers remained in their seats, still strapped in, fearful to move until given instructions to do so. Opposite him, the colour had drained from Dana's face and her normal olive complexion had turned to a ghostly pallor. A soldier boarded the helicopter and beckoned all of the passengers to stand and follow him. They dutifully did so, filing out of the giant transport and down its ramp. They emerged onto a runway at what was clearly a military base. Colin looked around as they were taken towards a waiting bus. They appeared to be on the outskirts of the city; Colin could see skyscrapers on the horizon, and a huge column of smoke was rising from their direction. The hotel, thought Colin, and a little shiver ran down his back.

He looked around. Sarah was ahead of him in the queue to board the bus, her arm around Dana's shoulders. "You did everything you could," he heard her telling Dana. He saw Dana nod in response, for once, meekly.

Aftermath

The early morning air was cool and crisp as they solemnly trooped out to the RAF's slate grey A330. An officer welcomed each one of them aboard as they boarded the aircraft. Dana once again found herself in a strange role reversal and shook her head in wonder at the turn of events over the last few days.

"Welcome aboard, Ma'am," said the officer.

Dana shook his hand. "Nice plane," she observed from her vantage point at the top of the steps, casting her eyes along the Airbus's sleek fuselage, with the Air Force roundels standing out starkly against the plain background.

The officer grinned. "You're in luck, this is normally the prime minister's plane."

Dana pulled a face. "What? That asshole?"

The officer looked around to check that nobody was listening and then leaned in conspiratorially. "That, ahem, asshole is currently in the process of breaking off diplomatic relations with these guys." He waved his arm vaguely around the general direction of the base, the ocean and the city.

Dana raised an eyebrow.

"International outcry," said the officer. "More human rights abuses in one night than we'd see in most wars in a year. The international community isn't standing for it. The UN's involved, sanctions are coming into place. It's going to be a real shit show here for quite some time to come. We're the last relief flight out of here."

"And after that?" Dana asked.

"My guess is they go back to being a virtually closed society. Don't bother us and we won't bother you. They've done their experiment with introducing foreigners and a few civil rights, and I don't think they liked the results."

"They came through for us though."

The officer nodded agreement. "Well, they would. It was good publicity for them to sweep to the rescue of a group of foreigners. But, unfortunately for them, that credit can't undo the massive debits from the killings during the riots."

Dana nodded and moved into the cabin. She took a seat behind Sarah and Rachel. She buckled up her seatbelt, relaxed into her seat and closed her eyes. In her mind's eye she was already on a beach, cocktail in hand and flirting with the waiters. Time, she thought, for some proper Dana Time.

Endgame

He looked up, as he always did when he heard the sound of an aircraft climbing into the air. He squinted into the early morning sun and saw the light glinting off one of the plane's wings. For a moment he was wistful, imagining himself in the cockpit, in the left hand seat, the city and ocean spread out below him. He imagined himself conversing with Air Traffic Control and could almost see the numbers on the digital altimeter ticking up as they gained height.

His daydream was interrupted by a shrill whistle. With his fellow prisoners, he started to move across the exercise yard towards the door that would take them back to their cells. As the line moved slowly forward towards the darkness that awaited them, Rob Mitchell craned his neck for one last look at the departing Airbus.

Acknowledgements

All my life, I've wanted to write a novel and now, as I approach my half-century, I have finall succeeded. I'm under no illusions that *Besieged* is a great work of literature, but I hope tha others will enjoy the story and find it a worthwhile read.

The genesis of *Besieged* was in a hotel a long way from home in the summer of 2019. I'd lik to thank the anonymous flight crew who were sitting on a table behind ours in the bar on evening for providing me with the inspiration for some of the characters. I'd also like to sa thanks to my cousin Adam and his wife Ashley for showing us around their city, which provided the background for the events in the novel.

I need to say a big thanks to the folks and communities at the National Novel Writing Month project. Without the catalyst that NaNoWriMo provided, I *may* eventually have written a novel, but it's extremely doubtful! If you have ever wanted to write a novel, why not check out their website at www.nanowrimo.org – but make sure you blank out the month of November to write it!

But my biggest thanks go to my four proof readers, Piers McLeish, Clare McInerney, Jo Schumacher and my wonderful wife, Allison Winstanley. They all gave me great encouragement and, most importantly, constructive feedback. All four commented on different elements of the book, so their feedback was much appreciated. Thanks guys!

And thank you to you, reader, for buying *Besieged*! I hope you enjoy it!

Jason Winstanley

Chester, UK

May 2020

Printed in Great Britain
by Amazon

24282392R00071